Act Like
You K

Also by Stephanie Perry Moore

Perry Skky Jr. series

Prime Choice
Pressing Hard
Problem Solved
Prayed Up
Promise Kept

Beta Gamma Pi series

Work What You Got
The Way We Roll

Act Like You Know

A Beta Gamma Pi Novel
Book 3

Stephanie Perry Moore

Dafina
Books

KENSINGTON PUBLISHING CORP.
www.kensingtonbooks.com

For
Dr. Deborah C. Thomas,
Dr. Paulette C. Walker,
Cynthia Boyd,
and
Christine Nixon

(the last four Southern Regional Directors for my
beloved Delta Sigma Theta Sorority Inc.)

You have all schooled me!
Thanks to your leadership and love,
I know I'm dynamic and empowered.
Under your guidance, you encouraged me
and many others to soar toward excellence.
May all readers, Greek or not,
know they are extraordinary and act like it.

ACKNOWLEDGMENTS

Going to college for reasons other than getting an education was my story. I thought I was ready to get out of my parents' home. I wanted to party. I couldn't wait to make my own rules. I was extremely excited to make new friends, and I was over-the-top loaded down with extracurricular activities: the dance team, football hostessing duties, college ambassador, Student Government Association chairperson, Homecoming Court, and Greek life. My grades weren't my first priority, and they weren't as great as they could have been because of this. Truthfully I barely had the grade point average to pledge. Though I was well rounded, I was not focused. To be the best collegiate student one can be, you must remember you're in school to learn. If there is nothing in your head, how can you help an organization? And once you gain that knowledge, you can have an even better life.

Writing a book on the importance of education wasn't easy. It's hard admitting that I personally should have done better. Yeah, I turned out okay, but being average was not my best. And I've created a harder road because of it. My **grand**parents didn't go to college, and they wanted me **to be** better than them. I want every young reader to be better than I am. And if my story helps you do better, hear me when I say I wish I had my master's and doctorate. I wish I would have soaked up everything my college studies had to

viii Acknowledgments

offer. I wish I would have had better grades so I could have been able to do more. You still have a chance to seize the moment. Don't hold yourself back. Act like you're there to become phenomenal. Here is a shout of thanks to those who helped me succeed despite my shortcomings:

For my family: parents, Dr. Franklin and Shirley Perry Sr.; brother, Dennis; sister-in-law, Leslie; and mother-in-law, Ms. Ann. For my extended family: Reverend Walter and Marjorie Kimbrough, Bobby and Sarah Lundy, Antonio and Gloria London, Cedric and Nicole Smith, Harry and Nino Colon, and Brett and Loni Perriman—your love teaches me how to give. Keep loving hard. I'm more compassionate because of your support.

For my publisher, Kensington/Dafina Books, and especially to the person who signed this series, Selena James— your knowledge of the publishing world helps make me better. Keep believing in me. I'm a more effective author because of your involvement.

For my writing team: Ciara Roundtree, Chantel Morgan, Ashley Morgan, Alyx Pinkston, Jenell Clark, Cassandra Brown, Dorcas Washington, Vanessa Davis Griggs, Victoria Christopher Murray, Sonya Jenkins, Edythe Woodruff, Beverly Jenkins, Joy Nixon, Chandra Dixon, Bridget Fielder, and Myra Brown Lee—your honesty helps me keep the story real. Keep staying on me. I'm humbled to have you as part of my team.

For my National Commission on Arts & Letters commit-
tee, particularly Yolanda Rodgers-Howsie, Dayna Fleming,
Anitra Shaw, and Denise Gilmore—your commitment to
the arts inspires me. Keep supporting dreams. I'm happy
to help others create because we're actively redefining together.

For my growing kids: Dustyn Leon, Sydni Derek, and
Sheldyn Ashli—your curiosity keeps me on my toes.
Keep wanting to know more. I pray you keep giving God
your all.

For my hubby, Derrick Moore—your quest for knowledge helps me not stay complacent. Keep treading new
ground. I'm doing God's will as I follow you.

For my readers—your faith that this book can bless you
warms my soul. Keep turning the page. I'm happy you've
chosen my novel.

And for my Lord and Savior, Jesus Christ, Your word is a
light unto my feet. Keep guiding my path. I'm following.

BETA GAMMA PI
TRADITIONS, CUSTOMS, & RITES

Founding Data

Beta Gamma Pi was founded in 1919 on the campus of Western Smith College by five extraordinary women of character and virtue.

Sorority Colors

Sunrise lavender and sunset turquoise are the official colors of Beta Gamma Pi. The colors symbolize the beginning and the end of the swiftly passing day and remind each member to make the most of every moment.

Sorority Pin

Designed in 1919, the pin is made of the Greek letters Beta, Gamma, and Pi. This sterling silver pin is to be worn over the heart on the outermost garment. There are five stones in the Gamma: a ruby representing courageous leadership, a pink tourmaline representing genuine sisterhood, an emerald representing a profound education, a purple amethyst representing deep spirituality, and a blue sapphire representing unending service.

Anytime the pin is worn, members should conduct themselves with dignity and honor.

The B Pin

The B Pin was designed in 1920 by the founders. This basic silver pin in the shape of the letter B symbolizes the beginning step in the membership process. The straight side signifies character. The two curves mean yielding to God and yielding to others. It is given at the Pi Induction Ceremony.

Sorority Flower

The lily is the sorority flower and it denotes the endurance and strength the member will need to be a part of Beta Gamma Pi for a lifetime.

Sorority Stone

The diamond is the sorority stone which embodies the precious and pure heart needed to be a productive member of Beta Gamma Pi.

Sorority Call

Bee-goh-p

Sorority Symbol

The eagle is the symbol of Beta Gamma Pi. It reflects the soaring greatness each member is destined to reach.

Sorority Motto

A sisterhood committed to making the world greater.

The Pi Symbol

The Bee insect is the symbol of the Pi pledges. This symbolizes the soaring tenacity one must possess to become a full member of Beta Gamma Pi.

Contents

1. Barrier   1

2. For   13

3. Pressure   24

4. Breach   34

5. Gasp   44

6. Pertinent   54

7. Bicker   64

8. Goal   75

9. Pierced   85

10. Broken   94

11. Gesture   102

12. Persuasive   113

13. Bombarded   123

14. Grind   133

15. Probation   143

16. Building   154

17. Graduate   163

18. Promise   173

BARRIER

"Alyx Cruz in the house. I'm a Beta Gamma Pi girl—get out the way! Alyx Cruz in the house. I'm a Beta Gamma Pi girl—I work it all day!" I chanted as I swayed my Latina hips from left to right at the National Convention's collegiate party for my beloved sorority, Beta Gamma Pi.

I wasn't trying to be funny or anything, but as a Mexican in a black sorority, it was not easy. I had it going on. The looks I got from men told me they wanted to get with me, and the looks I got from girls told me they wanted to be me, or they hated me because they weren't. It wasn't my fault that I didn't have kinky hair and that mine flowed more like a white girl's (though, truth be told, some days I wished mine was kinky—maybe then I'd fit in with everyone). Though they couldn't see it, I felt like a true sister from my core. But most Betas felt a

Spanish girl shouldn't be in a predominantly African American sorority. If they'd take time to get to know me they'd see I was down for the same things they were. That's why I joined Beta Gamma Pi.

However, if another one of my sorors looked at me like they wanted to snatch my letters off my chest, they were gonna be in for war—a real fight. I hated that I'd had to transfer to a new school. I'd finally gotten people to like me for me back in Texas, but because I'd partied just a little too much—okay, well, not just a little too much, a lot too much—my grades had suffered. And I'd put my scholarship in jeopardy. It was a minority scholarship, for which you had to maintain a 3.0 grade point average. I'd had to find another school that would take me with my 2.6 GPA, but I'd wished I could fix my mistakes. I hoped I wouldn't squander another great opportunity.

Now I was gonna have to start all over again winning friends at Western Smith College, my Tio Pablo's alma mater. My uncle helped my mom and me come to the United States from Mexico when I was three. He'd died when I was six, and it had been me and my mom ever since. My mom kept his framed degree in our house to inspire me to do more. So I applied to Western Smith and thankfully got enough financial aid to attend.

I couldn't get an education any other way. I had an opportunity, and I couldn't be crazy with it. I had to make sure I seized the chance. Here I was in America living the dream, and I had been about to waste all that. But now at Western Smith, I had a second chance.

But I couldn't focus on any of that, particularly when my favorite song came on. "Hey, get 'em up, get 'em up!"

I started shouting as I turned, swiveled, sashayed, and bumped into that girl Malloy I'd met an hour before.

"I am so sorry," I stuttered, taken back at seeing Malloy with about fifteen of her buddies all staring hard at me like I'd stolen their men or something.

"Oh, no, you're fine. It's perfect anyway. I was just telling my chapter sorors here about you," Malloy said in an overly sweet tone.

All these girls were from the Alpha chapter at Western Smith, where my sorority was founded. For some reason the girls in this chapter really thought they were better than everybody else. I could tell by the way they looked at me that they wished I'd go crawl under a rock. But I was on my way to their campus, and I already had my letters, so they needed to get over themselves. I looked at them, my hand on my hip and my eyes fully awake, like, "What . . . what you gon' do?"

"*Okayyy,* let's have some hugs and some love," Malloy said as she pushed me toward them.

The hugs I got from some of the girls made me want to throw up. They were so fake with it. When I got to the last few, I didn't even move to hug them. I wasn't a pledge. They could respect me or keep stepping. A few of the girls turned their noses up at me and walked off. I didn't care, because the sorors I pledged with would always be there for me when I needed sisterhood.

Then Malloy touched my shoulder and whispered, "Wait, please let me introduce you. Please."

Something in her gesture got to me. I didn't know her from Adam, but she was genuine. I really appreciated her wanting to make the awkwardness dissolve.

"These are my line sisters Torian and Loni"—neither girl standing next to her said hello—"our Chapter President, Hayden Grant; Bea, our First Vice President, and Sharon." Those three didn't even put up our sign, which was customary when you met a new soror.

"Now y'all, for real, you're being rude," Malloy scolded as she turned her back to me and tried to get her chapter sorors straight.

She didn't have to go defending me. I could hold my own. Shoot, they didn't want me in their chapter. Well, too doggone bad. I was coming, and what were they going to do about it?

But then, as I saw them continuously staring, I realized they were seriously feeling threatened. They didn't know me or my heart. I had to make them feel comfortable and let them know I wasn't trying to mess up their game. So I said, "Hey, I know it's tough accepting an outsider into your fold, but in my soul let me say I feel like family. I mean, I am your soror. I know a lot of Betas who aren't really excited about Spanish girls, but trust me, I don't want the spotlight, and my letters didn't come easy—I was hazed. I just want us to be cool, all right?"

Bea smiled and stuck out her hand for me to dap. When the others girls smiled as well—I guess now they knew I wasn't paper—we were cool.

"To me, more importantly than how I pledged is why I pledged," I continued sincerely. "I plan to make a difference in the community and I love this organization. Just give me a chance."

All the girls finally gave me a real embrace. I didn't

know where we'd go from here, but I was excited to find out.

I was in my hotel room with several other girls from my Texas chapter, trying to get some much needed rest after a long night, when the phone rang.

"Hello?" I said grumpily as I moved my line sister out of the way. I looked at the clock and was a little agitated that it was seven in the morning. I had just gotten in at three. "Who is it, and what do you want?"

In an irritatingly pleasant voice, a girl said, "Hey, sorry. I know it's early, but I'm looking for Alyx Cruz."

"Yeah, yeah, this is Alyx," I said, trying to sound a little more polite when I realized someone was trying to reach me.

"This is Malloy from last night. You know, from Alpha chapter?"

"Hey, I thought I recognized your voice. I'm sorry. We're just all tired over here."

"Well, I understand. We're just meeting with the National President in a bit, and all the sorors felt that since you're coming to our chapter, you'd like to be a part of the meeting. But it's going to be in fifteen minutes, so if you're too tired . . ."

"Where is the National President?" I said, my interest piqued.

Malloy responded, "Her room is the penthouse suite."

Really psyched, I said, "Oh, for real? I'll be right there. Wow, you all are meeting with the National President? How cool. Thanks for wanting me to come."

"Well, it's not going to be a good meeting."

"I don't understand," I said as I searched for some clothes.

Malloy explained in a dejected tone, "That hazing you were talking about last night that you went through, how you earned your letters? Well, we've been caught with quite a bit of it."

"Oh, okay. Got you. We might be suspended from Western Smith," I said, feeling like I was going to be in for a crazy ride. "See you in a bit."

We hung up, and I stepped over a couple more of my line sisters. I couldn't believe we had so many in the hotel. It was supposed to be only four of us in a room, tops, and we were double that. And I swear as I stepped over a couple bodies that it seemed like we had picked up some extra stragglers. Looking around the room, I knew I was gonna have to buckle down and figure out what it was I wanted to do with my life because I had to get paid one day. I couldn't live like I had all my days. Seeing my mom working two jobs to make ends not even meet just wasn't cool. If having money could afford me a better lifestyle, I needed to get myself together so I could have better choices. Meeting with the National President of our organization seemed like a step in the right direction because, let's face it, it wasn't all about what you knew, it was about who you knew. Being around a dynamic leader could be only a positive experience, even if the chapter was in trouble.

Thinking this would be a great experience went right out the window when I saw firsthand how upset the National President was about the mess Alpha chapter was in. I walked in the room, and she started going off on the Alpha chapter girls. No one was smiling. Malloy had warned me.

"There is no more negotiating. I don't want to hear anything else. You guys are off the yard, and there will not be a line this year. Don't even think about doing anything underground or crooked, or I will make sure I take your letters for good," President Murray stated boldly.

"Malloy, say something!" Bea said as if Malloy had some influence with the lady.

"Excuse me, young lady, I know that's my daughter—"

I almost choked. I hadn't known Malloy's mom was the National President. How cool was that? Malloy *did* have influence.

The National President spoke with sternness. "But Malloy is in a chapter that participated in some things that are illegal. No one can change Western Smith's ruling that left Beta Gamma Pi suspended for one year, and no one will change my mind giving the same sanction. Unless we not go for two years?"

"Mom!" Malloy called out in a merciful cry, wanting her mother to take it easy.

"Listen, I'm not going to argue any of this with you guys. The rules are clearly stated, and you all signed papers saying you would not participate in or keep from the National Headquarters, also known as the Grand Chapter, any hazing, hitting, mental abuse, or anguish and the like, and though I know some of you will get harder punishment than others, you guys are on probation this year. No dances, no Beta week—none of that. Focus on your academics because I've looked at your grades, and they've dropped!" Then she looked my way. "Young lady, what's your name?"

"I'm Alyx Cruz. I'm transferring from a school in Texas."

She smiled and nodded. "So you have a new addition to your sorority, almost like having a line of one. You guys take this new blood and work together. Let's do the right thing. You need to focus on bonding, going to training workshops, and public service events. Then next year we'll revisit, and if you've complied and there are no more infractions, maybe I'll reverse this decision."

A couple girls were crying. Everyone was angry, including Malloy. Just my luck. I was coming to a chapter that was suspended. Oh, well, we'd find another way to have a stellar year. I wanted to get to know the National President better, but she was in no mood after laying down the law, so I exchanged cell-phone numbers with Malloy, Torian, and Loni and went back down to my hotel room to pack up my stuff to head home. Being in Alpha chapter was really going to be a trip.

Two weeks passed, and those weeks had actually been difficult. I really hated leaving my mom down in El Paso. She seemed so weak and frail. Something was going on with her, but she told me she'd be okay and sent me on my way.

Because going to summer school at Western Smith had been a last-minute decision to help me get acclimated early in my new school, I didn't have a place to stay. But the sorors had come through! After calling some of the

Alpha chapter sorors, it was arranged for Torian and Loni to let me crash at their place. Word was Malloy had stayed with them a while last semester. I couldn't believe some of the stories all the sorors were telling me that had gone on with this chapter. No wonder they were suspended. A soror from another school had actually passed away because of a severe hazing incident? Another girl had lost a baby in the same crazy car crash? A female had stalked Malloy and destroyed her property? This place was not going to be boring for me, for sure.

I was in the bathroom at Torian and Loni's getting ready. I had a date. I had been on campus for less than nine days, and I already had a hot tie from the basketball team ready to hook up with me.

I started hurrying when I noticed the time. My date was going to be here any minute. But I was distracted when voices outside the bathroom door got louder. What were the roomies into it about?

Loni fumed, "Well, if you told her she could have company, she should have cleaned up this place first. She's got our apartment looking like a hot mess."

I leaned my head on the back of the door. Okay, I had to admit I wasn't the cleanest person in the world, but there was no need for people to raise their voices and get all upset and everything. I'd straighten things up later.

Torian said, "Okay, but I didn't think you'd be mad. She can clean up later."

Exactly, I thought.

"I'm just not up for company, okay? Shoot, it's been a minute since I broke up with my man, and now she's having company?"

"Well, that's just the thing," Torian said in a odd voice.

What was the thing? I wondered. What did Loni's breakup have to do with me and my new stud baller?

"What do you mean 'That's just the thing'?" Loni asked, reading my mind.

Then there was a knock at the front door. I looked in the mirror and left the bathroom. They could keep talking, but I had to entertain.

Not looking at either of them, I said, "I got it, girls! Sorry I didn't tidy up enough."

"I didn't mean for you to hear me, but because you did, this looks pretty junky. Now you got company coming over. This makes us look bad. We don't live like slobs," Loni said.

"I'm sorry!" The knock came a little louder. "Coming, babe!"

"You don't even know him, and you're calling him 'babe,' " Loni said, aggravated at everything I did.

Quickly I told her, "Girl, it's just a figure of speech. Relax. You ain't my mama."

"If I was, I'd make you clean up after yourself a little bit better than you're doing," Loni said, rolling her eyes.

I opened up the door and gave Ronnie, the six-foot-four-and-a-half, fine specimen standing in front of me, a big hug. He smelled good, and he had the prettiest smile. Loni wasn't gonna disturb my groove even if he and I had to take our fun somewhere else.

"Oh, no, you didn't!" Loni said from behind me, even more upset.

"What? I can't hug him either?" I said, really confused.

Ronnie looked at her in a very weird way. The two of

them definitely had a vibe going on. I was caught in the middle, and I didn't know what to say about anything.

"Okay, Torian, I can't believe you would do this to me," Loni said to her girl. "And how could you come to my place and see another girl?" Loni said to Ronnie.

"Oh, you know him?" I asked, trying to sort it all out.

Loni's eyes welled up. Now I knew this was the other thing Torian had been referring to. Loni turned and walked away.

Torian went after her. "Y'all had broken up. I didn't think it was any big deal."

He came in, took my hand, and said, "Forget them. She used to be my girl, but you know—no big deal."

Jerking my arm away, I said, "Hold up, I wasn't trying to cause that kind of confusion up in here. I mean, she is my soror. They let me stay here. I just met you the other night. I didn't realize it was all that. I don't think this is a good idea."

"Wait, you ain't even gonna see me? I had plans and stuff for us."

"I understand, but sorry." I opened the door and shoved him right out of it.

Then I went into the room and saw Loni crying fully. "Hey, I'm sorry, Loni."

"It's fine. I'm just disrespected all over the place."

"Well, I didn't think you would be mad!" Torian said.

"What do you mean?" Loni asked. "Alyx didn't know I went out with him, but he did, and so did you. And that's why I dropped his tail because he is inconsiderate. But, Torian, you're supposed to be my girl. Don't you know that hurts? How you gonna let a man I used to get with come up in my house to visit somebody else? Please, y'all both need to get out. I knew we shouldn't have let her stay here."

"Hey, again, I'm sorry. You said yourself I didn't know. He's gone."

"Whatever. Just go," Loni said as she pushed us out of her room and slammed the door.

Torian just sat on the couch depressed. I had created a mess and didn't know how to fix it. As hard as I tried, I had to get along with these new people, but there was still a big barrier.

2

FOR

I felt horrible that I had caused such a big rift between two roommates, two sorors, two friends. So I walked to the hall closet, got out my suitcase, and began packing my things. Yeah, their couch was comfortable and all, but the tension I had caused was way too thick. For real, I didn't know Ronnie had previously dated Loni.

I was making the right choice though because now tears were streaming down Torian's pitiful face. I knew she felt horrible that she had let her friend down. She was hurting, and that certainly hadn't been my intent. I had already apologized and had immediately kicked the guy out, yet Loni was furious. Seemed logical to me that if I left for good as well, they could resolve some issues and heal.

"Where are you going?" Torian said when she saw me packing my stuff.

"I don't know. It's not like I have someplace to lay my head. I'll be all right. I do believe things work out. Somehow they always do. I'm not sweating stuff like that."

"You not sweating where you're going to live? We can't just let you go." She went and banged on Loni's door. "Open up! You got to come out. Alyx is going to leave."

There was no response. I wasn't surprised. I knew Loni was pissed. She couldn't deal with me right now; she was working on her own hang-ups. Having no hard feelings on my part, I kept packing. Bottom line, I had to do what I had to do.

"I'm sorry about all this," Torian said as she helped me place things into my bag.

For a girl who wondered where I was going, she certainly wasn't trying too hard to keep me with her. I really wasn't in the mood for hearing her whine and go on and on and on about how bad she felt for letting Loni down. However, I didn't have a choice: I had to gather my stuff together, and she was talking, so I had to listen.

"I love her. I would never try to hurt her. I mean, yeah, I saw Ronnie talking to you, but I thought they were over."

"Okay, let me just school you," I said when I finally got fed up hearing her act like she had no clue why her friend was really ticked. "It's just a code, you know? You just got to treat people how you'd like to be treated. You say you know her really well. So then you know she probably still likes that guy. I mean, the dude is fine. Why do you think I was trying to get with him? And me talking to him is one thing, because you don't have nothing to do with that, but allowing me to bring him to her place, her space, that's foul. To her, you placed a knife in her back."

Torian stopped packing, gripped her head, and said, "But she was through with him."

"Um, yeah, but not really. Why would she be all freaking out like that?"

"Wow, I see what you're saying."

"Yeah, sister lessons come when you live with them. Just learn from your mistakes and be better next time. Think how it would affect a girl before you make a decision. And who knows, Ronnie might have been playing me to make her jealous anyway."

"That's pretty cool of you to think that," Torian said to me. "Look how cute you are. All the dudes around here have been talking about you the last couple weeks—'Who's y'alls new soror?' 'When are you going to introduce me to your new soror?' 'I like the Spanish chick.' "

"I'm just Alyx, okay? Yes, I'm different and I'm new, but the novelty will wear off. I think I just like to have fun, and I just don't take everything so seriously. So many girls—so many of our sorors—stress out too much, and men hate that. Let go and feel confident. They'll come flying to you, trust me."

"You know what, I got an idea." Torian reached over and gave me a hug. "Thank you. I'm going to work it out with Loni, but I think I know where you can go."

"Huh?" I was real confused then.

About fifteen minutes later when I was all packed, Malloy showed up. She was smiling. I hadn't seen her since the conference.

Malloy said, "Hey, girl, this is going to be perfect. I

need somebody to stay at my place while I go to New York. You down for it?"

"Yeah, I can house-sit for sure," I said as I got my suitcase and walked out of my bedroom, happy I was not going to be homeless.

Loni cracked open her door. She didn't come out, but I could tell she sort of wanted to say something to me. It was a weird place we were in; I had hurt her unintentionally. So I broke the ice by going over to her door and saying, "Listen, I'm sorry about all this. You don't have to worry—I won't be talking to him anymore. And Torian really does feel bad. She gets that she crossed the line. Forgive her."

"You really don't have to leave," Loni said as she fully opened her door.

"I appreciate that, but I think you two need to work your thing out. I'm going to have a place all to myself. Maybe you can come visit."

"Thanks. Bye, girl," Loni said as I walked myself out the front door.

When we got to Malloy's place, it was new and upgraded with the finest of everything—even a granite countertop in the kitchen.

"Your folks must be loaded," I said when I laid eyes on the new, furnished, upscale pad.

Modestly Malloy said, "My dad's got a little penny."

"And you're going to New York?"

"Yes, I'm going to work with a designer. My man just got drafted with the Giants, and he worked it all out."

"The awesome player from Southwestern Arkansas? Wait, that's your guy? Dang, I need to be getting in your suitcase and going with you."

"Maybe you'll come to a game sometime this year, but for now I'm just thankful you're going to be here. I had such trouble last semester with my place."

"Yeah, I remember Torian and Loni telling me all about it. I'll make sure nobody takes anything."

"I don't need to do no background check on you, do I?" Malloy teased.

I joked back, "You better."

"Seriously though, no wild parties. I really don't want nobody over here but you. I'm sorry, I know that sounds cruel. I mean, Loni, Torian, some of the sorors are cool. But nobody I don't know. And no dudes. I just . . . no."

"Oh, no, your house, your rules. No problem. For free rent I can accommodate."

"All right, girl. Thanks for helping me work this out."

The summer session was weighing me down. If it wasn't one test, it was some paper I had to do. Ugh, I hated school, and I knew I needed to get my attitude changed. Dang though—why was education so important? I mean, this was a summer session, for goodness' sake. We were supposed to have a little fun.

So that's when I hooked up with Bea and Trisha. They were about to be seniors. I loved their no-holds-barred attitude. We couldn't have any parties as Betas on our campus—so we went to find sorors in chapters close by and partied with them.

"Thanks y'all for picking me up. Malloy's house has everything, but sometimes the novelty of being alone wears off," I said as I got in the back of Bea's ride.

Before we went to the party we stopped off at a convenience store on some dark country road in Arkansas. I was hungry and thirsty and didn't have a dime to my name. But that was not gonna stop me from taking care of business.

"I just got money for gas, that's all," Trisha said.

"And I just got a couple dollars to get us in the party. What you going in the store for, Alyx? You got some money?" Bea asked.

Swatting my hand, I walked toward the store and said, "Girls, what y'all want? I got this."

"Oh, dang. You rolling like that? Hook us up then," Bea said.

Trisha nodded. "Yeah, hook us up."

I was going to work my charm. You know, flirt a little bit, get the cashier to go on and let me have a few goodies. But how come the seventy-year-old, mean-looking white woman had to be in there? What was a girl to do?

"Can I help you?" she asked in the most insincere way I'd ever heard.

"Uh, where's your restroom, ma'am?" I asked, making her think I didn't want any merchandise.

As I contemplated my next move, the phone behind the desk rang. Before picking it up, the woman pointed to the restroom. Slowly I walked back there, and thankfully somebody started talking her ear off. She got into some long conversation, and I could hear the four-pack of wine coolers and the large bag of chips just calling my name. I ran track in high school. So I opened up the case, put the four-pack under my arm, grabbed the bag of chips, and was headed out the door until I saw a pack of M&M's. The cashier had her back to me; she wasn't even looking at me. But I just had to have the M&M's, so I grabbed them and jetted out the door.

"Go! Go! Go!" I yelled, taking no chances. "Start the car—go!" I jumped in the backseat, and Bea sped off.

"Okay, wait, what you got me all involved in?" Bea turned around and yelled to the back of the car.

"Oh, please, you said you were thirsty."

"Yeah, and you said you had it."

"I do have it. Here." I handed Bea a strawberry daiquiri. "You want some chips and some M&M's, too? I know you want some M&M's." I leaned into the front of the car. "Doesn't matter how I got it."

Bea said, "Yeah, it does matter how you got it. The police may come after us."

"The police? Are you kidding? Girl, please, that little country store ain't going to be able to identify nobody. Sometimes when you don't have what you want, you can't just stop, you got to overcome obstacles. Isn't that what the sorority teaches us? We got to push through, persevere, get it done by any means necessary. Come on, you better act like you know how to work it."

"Girl, please," Bea said. "I don't believe in stealing. That's not at all a part of what the sorority teaches us. Are you kidding? All that stuff will come back to you. Tell 'em, Trisha."

"Yeah, I've been there. I got caught taking chapter money," Trisha said in a solemn voice. "I'd give anything to erase what I did, and I did it to pay my tuition. Still wasn't right."

Wow, that was news. However, I couldn't let her stay down. I handed her a wine cooler also.

"Go on and drink it—you know you want to," I said to Trisha.

Trisha looked over at Bea and said, "She gave it to me. I didn't steal it."

"Yeah, whatever. You can look at it any way you need to to make yourself feel better," Bea said.

"But you thirsty, and you got something to drink, something that's going to make you have a lot of fun at the dance. So it's just a little wine cooler; it's just something to munch on. Enjoy it. Don't worry about how I got it." I turned around and I looked behind us. It was pitch black. Nobody coming for us. Though it was wrong, it was all good.

"Girl, you are crazy," Bea said as she held her hand out for an M&M.

"Crazy ain't never killed nobody."

"You're a bad influence, that's what you are. Open up my cooler," Bea said to Tricia as we pulled into the full parking lot.

She was saying she wasn't for it, but her actions were for it. Maybe I *was* a bad influence. That sort of bothered me. But what was wrong with having a little wild side?

Five days later I had gotten completely over feeling guilty for being the bad girl around town. I mean, shucks, it was summertime, hot as I don't know what in Arkansas. Dang, I had been so good at Malloy's place; I had invited just a few of my classmates to study. They weren't sorors, but certainly studying wasn't going to be a bad thing.

However, I was really shocked and probably got what I deserved when the classmates invited some locals who didn't even go to school at Western Smith. They came in twenty strong with loud music, beer, and cigarettes, and I was stunned when I saw one guy with some weed.

Grabbing the ring leader, Vince, I said, "Okay, so, wait, you guys can't bring anybody else up in here. This is a study party. You know, like an unwind party, like just a few of us. This isn't even my place. No, this ain't going to start before it even gets started."

Vince said, "Oh, relax, Lex."

"Lex?" I said, looking at him like he didn't know me that well.

"Here, take a beer. It's just my cousin and his homies trying to set the mood right. We're going to study. What you want to study? Five times five is twenty-five," Vince said, showing me he was tipsy. If I couldn't beat them, I would join them. So I took the beer, sat down, and chugged it. I just wanted all my cares to go away. I did hate school, but yet I had to be here. I had only one class, and it wasn't like I was acing it. My mind always seemed to go to other places, and all I wanted to do was enjoy life. Why did it have to be so stressful?

I went over to the stereo, turned up the music, and just started dancing. Everybody started screaming. Life was too hard; we were just college students. If we didn't enjoy life now, when would we ever be able to enjoy it? Pretty soon after this would come jobs, spouses, kids, and responsibilities. Even if I failed college, I was going to look wistfully back on those college days and the blast I had.

The upscale, cute apartment was starting to become a little less adorable. Pictures that had been hanging perfectly were now tilted. The walls that had been a pretty beige and gold were now filled with handprints. A few glasses that had been put neatly in the cupboard were now broken on the floor. I could clean it all up, but where was I going to find money to buy paint and replace those glasses? Well, now wasn't the time to worry about it.

So I started screaming, "Let's have fun—it's a party!"

The door opened, and more people came in. I welcomed them with open arms until I was stunned to see Malloy walk through last.

She screamed, "I trusted you, Alyx! You promised me you weren't going to have any parties at my house, and people are getting high on the stairs. What, you want the campus police to find out this is my place and I end up in jail?"

"Aw, girl, loosen up," I said, letting the alcohol speak for me as I patted her on the back.

"Ugh, you're drunk. I can't believe this. I can't believe I let Torian talk me into this. And to think I wasn't even coming home this weekend. My designer has a fashion show out of the country, and my man is away at training camp. So I'm like, let me just come home, get more acquainted with my new soror, enjoy my place. I was even thinking about asking you to live here this whole semester so I wouldn't have to be alone, because I'm still a little afraid of all that, and what do you go do? Blow it all, ignore everything I said, and just do whatever you wanted to. You ruined my place, and if you ain't got no money to stay nowhere, how you going to fix it up? How are you going to make this better?"

"E—everybody g—g—get out," I said, so angry things were getting out of control.

Nobody moved, but then Malloy started screaming about the police, and her apartment was empty in less then five minutes.

"Why, Alyx? You're a girl with so much going for you, and it's like you're just throwing it all away. Bea called me while I was up there and told me you stole something from a store. I just—I don't know. Our chapter does have a reputation. We're classy girls with high standards. We're selective and uppity for a reason. And now you're coming in cutting what we stand for."

3

PRESSURE

"Okay, so what's the big meeting about?" I said to Malloy at an emergency meeting at the Alpha chapter sorority room the next morning.

We had never finished our chat from the previous night. After the lashing she had been giving me, let's say I was through. I had been ready to leave, but she had told me to stay in the guest room. She'd woken me forty minutes ago and told me we needed to meet with everyone else. I wasn't crazy though—I knew she'd called her girls and snitched on me.

I had met most of the sorors from Alpha chapter during the National Convention when we'd been stuffed in the room with the National President as she'd told us our fate for the year. But there were still a few more sorors I had to meet, and it would have been nice if this had been a welcome breakfast party—you know, sorors all excited to meet the new chapter member—but the faces were all grim and stuffy. Some of them looked like they wanted to attack me.

I had no idea how they had gotten into so much trouble with the hazing. They seemed so rigid, like they had something stuck up their behinds that needed to come out so they could breathe, enjoy life, just live out loud. These girls seemed like they never broke the rules. But who were they fooling? The chapter was suspended because of their crazy actions. So no matter what they thought of me, they weren't too different.

"Alyx, um, we need to have a serious conversation with you," Hayden Grant, the Chapter President, said to me as people got out of the way and I had a clear aisle to the front of the room.

As I looked around, I noticed what they had done to make their place look extra special. We had a room at my old campus, but it didn't have any of the rich history this Alpha chapter room had. The sorority had been founded in 1919—the black-and-white pictures of the five founders that adorned the wall were something special.

When I made it to the front, I wanted to tell them to chill out and have a little fun. However, I knew this was serious. So I looked at Hayden. I asked, "Yeah, what's going on? What do you need?"

"See, it's that attitude right there," Loni said, **obvi**ously still salty about Ronnie.

Bea said, "It's just a little too much for our chapter. You don't take any of this seriously. We called you here to tell you we all have a problem with you."

I rolled my eyes because Bea really didn't want me to

respond to that. I mean, what were they going to do—kick me out? Not. I had made a lifetime commitment. I wasn't going anywhere. Everybody wasn't going to like everybody all the time anyway—so what?

Hayden put up her hand like "I got this." What—she was going to try to tell me that in a nice way? Like there was any kind of polite way to tell me they thought I was too much for their chapter. So I looked away. I wasn't even going to give her the respect of looking her in the eye. They were all ganging up on me. There were, like, twentysomething of them in the room. Then Hayden sat down beside me.

"I know this has to sound a little crazy, and I'm sorry about that, but we do have high standards. We are Betas, for goodness' sake, Alyx. You can't be throwing parties where people bring drugs and stuff into one of your sorority sister's apartments."

I couldn't find Malloy in the crowd, but I couldn't wait to talk to her. Our business was our business. Why did she have to put our stuff out in the street like that? She got on me. I didn't need her betraying our confidence about stuff.

"And Malloy didn't tell us," Hayden said, as if she could read my thoughts. "We all got friends in different sororities and fraternities, and everybody knew what you did. The campus police were on their way over there to bust up the place. If Malloy hadn't sent everybody walking . . ."

"Yeah, people are going to be watching us this year," Bea said. "I mean, you know what you did when you were with Trisha and me."

"You liked it, and you kind of participated in it," I said, remembering her chugging the free cooler.

"Yeah, and I had regrets. Nobody wants you to go anywhere, but we do want you to chill," Bea said.

"Think about all of us collectively. We are a group, and we are only as strong as our weakest link."

"So don't be weak!" someone yelled out.

"If you got something to say to me, be woman enough to come up here like Hayden and say what you got to say!" I shouted. "Most people would think it's a little intimidating, all y'all trying to tell me something. It's not like I'm on drugs. It's not like I'm a drunk. It's not like I'm bringing down the sorority."

I heard a lot of huffs and hisses at that moment. Obviously most of them disagreed with that statement. But they did need to look in the mirror, and I was just the one to make them see they weren't known as the prima donnas anymore.

"All right, fine," I said, got up, and walked out, realizing that maybe I needed to look in the mirror as well.

As soon as I shut the door behind me, I laid my head on it. *Alyx, what are you doing? Don't be so much of a knucklehead that you can't learn. The doors are closing in on you, girl.* Now, I was torn.

"Do you even understand what I am saying to you, young lady?" said goofy-looking Dean Hue. It was noon, and I sat in his office at Minority Scholarships, getting a big lecture about my failing midterm grade.

Dean Hue said, "Hello? Hello? Are you even listening to me? Listen, I don't know what's going on in that mind of yours, young lady, but I can clearly see you're not paying me any attention. It's my job to keep students like you in school, but it's your job to stay here." He leaned in over his desk and distorted his weird face even more. "I pushed for you to be here. I spoke directly to your mother, who's struggling back there in Texas and pleaded for me to give you an opportunity. You had only one class, one probationary class you had to come up here and excel in, and you're failing it. Alyx, I was here with your uncle years back, and I want you to make it."

"The semester is not over, sir," I said, irritated that he was sweating me and trying to pull on my heartstrings by mentioning my uncle.

"I don't need the smart lip. You're not passing the class, and if you don't at least get a two-point-oh from this class, I'm not going to be able to keep you. One class—turn the grade around, or you don't need to get too comfortable. I see you applying for housing and all this other kind of financial support. Don't even push these papers through if this is the effort you plan to keep giving. Right now you're not holding up your end of the deal. If you're not going to try, if you're not going to apply yourself, maybe we just need to cut some things out now. Maybe that will give you some interest in what I have to say."

I was still looking around. Here he was, telling me my future here was all but gone, and I had no response. A part of me was so angry at myself.

It reminded me of my father, who had died trying to provide for his family; it had broken his heart when he'd pushed my mom and me to go to the United States without him. I have thick skin; I take a lot because I have been through a lot, and it seems like people are always getting at me for something. Even in all that and through all that, I still have dreams. I have goals, and I know the only way for me to accomplish them is to keep my butt in school. But why in the world am I not trying? Why in the world does it seem like I don't care? Because I do.

I finally murmured, "No, sir, I can do better. Please, please don't give up on me."

"Don't give up on yourself. I don't know what kind of school you think this is, but Partying 101 is not a major," he said.

Paranoid, I said, "Who told you I've been partying? What, my sorority sisters been coming over here talking?"

"Nobody's had to tell me. To get a grade like this, what else could you be doing? You have only one class. I don't know if you go to class at all, or if you go high, drunk, or just plain nonchalant. Something is going on with you, and you're asking me to give you another chance. You got to give me a reason why I should, because based on the way you've represented yourself in my office today, and your grades, I have no reason to have hope you are going to turn yourself around."

"I got to make something of myself. My uncle's last dying wish was for me to go to college and really make something of myself."

"Yeah, I remember your mother telling me something like that when I spoke to her. She was brokenhearted that you had already messed up one opportunity down in Texas and she was having to send you far away just so you could go to school. She cried to me about not having money of her own to pay for school. So for your uncle, your mom, yourself, why aren't you producing better results?"

Frustrated but respectful, I blurted, "It's hard. School doesn't come easy for me, all right?"

"I know it's tough and rough and hard, but you've got to open up a book. Get a tutor. Do something. We will go through until the end of the semester, and we will meet here after this class is over. If you don't have better than a C, you can't stay. But if you dig deep down inside yourself to the part that's talking to me now, maybe you do have a chance, Alyx Cruz. Maybe you do."

August in Arkansas wasn't as hot as it was in Texas, but it sure was close. Malloy's apartment complex had a swimming pool. I laid out later that day after dipping in some of the cool water for relief. I just looked up at the sky and said, "Are You even up there? If there is some kind of God, why in the world is my life so hard? Why is it so hard for me to do well in school? I can do it, but can You make it easier on me? Can't You take away this desire for me to want to party and have fun? I mean, not completely away, but just enough for me to focus? What am I talking about? I don't even know if You're really even up there."

"There you are," Malloy said as she rushed over to me with her cell phone in her hand.

"What? What? What's going on?" I sighed, waiting for the other shoe to drop.

"Telephone for you." She was all out of breath.

"Thanks."

"It's your mom."

"*Hola, Mami! ¿Cómo estás? Te extraño.*"

"*Te extraño también.*"

"Mom, why do you sound so jumbled? What's going on? Why can't I hear you? Talk to me, please."

"I'm okay, Alyx. What I am about to tell you is going to sound hard, but we are going to be okay."

I sat straight up and held my head to brace myself. "Mom, you're scaring me. Please talk to me. Tell me what's wrong."

"I have a brain tumor."

"A brain tumor!" I repeated, not even realizing Malloy was looking directly in my face as she sank down and started shaking in a panic on the bench by me. She must have heard my mom's uneasiness. Seeing her upset was even tougher to take.

I turned around the other way and whispered, "A brain tumor—no, Mom, you have headaches off and on. Everything has always been okay. You just take some BC and you'll be fine. No, you got to go see another doctor."

"I have seen two other doctors. They both say the exact same thing the first man said. They are giving me about six months to live."

"Mom, no!" My hands trembled, and my heart was in free-fall.

"I know, sweetie, I know. God needs me up there. I get to see your father and my mother and my grandmother and Adam and Eve, and, oh, I can't wait to see Eve. I got some things to talk to that girl about."

"Mom, this is not funny! This isn't a joke. You aren't going anywhere for a long time. I need you here. I need you. If there was a God, He wouldn't do something like this to you."

"It's actually been a blessing. I've been able to get my sister and her two kids over here for a temporary visa."

"I'm coming, Mom. I'm going back to Texas."

"No, no, I talked to that dean, the man that went out of his way to let you into the school, Alyx. You've got to work harder. You've got to try for me. If you don't want to get an education for yourself, do it for your dad. Do it for me."

"Mom, no. Please just tell me you are trying to motivate me. You're saying this so I'll work hard. I'll work hard, Mom, if you take it back. You don't have to make this up!"

"I'm not, and I would not hurt you and say this if it weren't true, but I need you to pray for Mommy. Pray that I can go through this transition with the same peace I feel in my heart now. Please take care of yourself. They say it can be six months, but it can be tomorrow—it could be next year. I just want you to know, Alyx, that you are precious. Not just on the outside, not just what the world sees. Please—you are gorgeous on the inside, too."

"Mom, I got to go. I'll call you later."

I hung up the phone, turned over on the beach chair, and cried. I was tough, but I wasn't that tough. Malloy touched my back.

"Your mom isn't going to be okay, is she?"

I sat up, and we both just cried. It was amazing that she cared like that. She barely knew me, and she didn't know my mom like that at all. I looked up to the sky again, so angry for what was going on. Malloy helped me up, but I fell to the ground. My mom not with me? This was too much.

"You can be strong, Alyx. For your mom, you have to be. Let's go home and think this through."

"Home—you haven't said anything to me in two days. I know you want me out," I said with the only ounce of strength I had.

"I want you around. If you can put up with me. We are sisters, and we need each other. We need to be able to forgive and be there for one another. Though I don't want any partying in my place, I need to get over it and be real. I don't want to be alone. And you are way cooler than all my other sorors," Malloy said, making me smile. "Don't tell them that though."

She hugged me, and I rose. I guess there was someone up above looking out. God knew I needed Malloy's support because without it I probably would have lost it. We made our way back to her—I mean, our—apartment. We were exhausted from the heat, emotionally tied to each other by the gripping news I'd received, and overwhelmed by all the pressure.

4

BREACH

"So her mom is dying?" I heard somebody ask outside my room.

I couldn't relax because of all the commotion outside my door, and though it had been only a few hours since I'd lain down, when I turned over and heard the voices, I knew Malloy had told somebody my business. I had a serious problem with that.

"Shhh, keep your voice down," I heard Malloy say.

"I just feel bad." I finally recognized that it was Loni's voice. "Here we are, we're all just getting on her, and now she's going through this crisis. This is horrible."

Okay, now I was even more upset. I didn't need anyone to take pity on me. This was my struggle, and I could deal with it alone. Malloy knew only because my mom had needed to get in touch with me, and I'd had to use her phone, but that didn't give her the right to spread my business to anybody. I got out of bed and paced back and forth.

I heard Torian say, "We called Hayden and everybody."

"No, tell me you didn't," Malloy said.

"Yeah, they're on their way."

"Okay, that's it!" I finally uttered as I opened the door, yanked Malloy inside, and slammed it shut. "What are you doing? Why are you telling everybody my business? Who's all coming over here? I can't believe you would do this to me. Is this your payback because I had a few people over to your place last week? I thought we had moved past that. Weren't we gonna be sisterly to each other, honor each other's wishes, and stay out of each other's affairs?"

"I'm sorry. I just called Torian and Loni. They're my girls, and I hate that this is happening to you. We're sisters, and we're supposed to support—"

"I don't need anybody to support me on this. It's not like anybody can go into my mom's body, play God, clean her up, get rid of the tumor, and make her all right. I mean, it is what it is. What you guys can do for me is leave me the heck alone."

"Okay, wait, now," Loni said on the other side of the door. "Don't be going off on her. Just 'cause you don't know how we roll around here."

"Hush," Torian said to Loni.

"Yeah, hush, Loni, I got this," Malloy said.

"That girl don't like me anyway, and you're going to call her and tell her my business?" I asked.

"I do like you. I do like you—it's just that—" I opened

the door. But before I could vent anymore, the doorbell rang, and not only was it Hayden and Bea, but Sharon and Dena and a couple other girls I didn't even know the names of yet. Hayden came straight over to me and put her arms around me. I stepped back. I mean, sisterhood was one thing, but we weren't close like that. There was no need to act like it was all good between us. Last time I'd seen these girls, they'd been dogging me out.

"I'm so sorry to hear about your mom," Hayden said, stepping farther into my space.

Malloy said, "I'm sorry, I know it's got to be hard. And I didn't mean to betray you, if that's how you feel. But we're here because we are one group. When one goes through something, we all got to go through it. You shouldn't have to go through this alone."

They all gave me the saddest looks. I just stared back. The mean stares I had gotten the day before from the chapter—those stares were gone. The sincerity in their faces, the pity they felt, the empathy—it was all real. I fell to my knees, thinking about my mom, what she was going through and the fact that this was real, and I guess I didn't need to go through it alone. I did appreciate that they cared. Though Malloy had crossed the privacy line, in my book, I guessed that was a blessing. It was just hard. I'd been telling them more about myself than I ever thought I would to anyone.

"My mother lost her job last year. I know that's caused her a ton of stress. Her best friend's family got deported last year. It's just been one thing after another, and she's been having these headaches, and who knew it was a tumor? Maybe if she would have gone to the doctor earlier, maybe if she'd . . ."

"You can't do any of that to yourself," Hayden encouraged. "We just got to let go and trust and pray that a miracle can happen. If we all collectively agree together, you don't know what God will do."

I hugged her tight. The walls I had built slowly came tumbling down. I had sisters, and I felt—no, I knew—they cared.

As I walked across the campus to meet some dumb tutor who was going to help me pass my summer class, I was severely agitated. I had had several tutors before in Texas, and none of them had ever helped me. They'd always been so arrogant, such know-it-alls. Never wanted to try to understand why I, a dummy, couldn't get what they knew to be easy. So, yeah, I had a chip on my shoulder. Just because they had been tutoring for free, they didn't have to act like it was my fault they didn't have a life. I mean, shucks, most of them were ugly anyway.

But not this time. It wasn't going to be easy to concentrate when the other person getting tutored was so fine.

"About time you got here," he said, snapping at me before he even asked me my name. "You are five minutes late."

"Five minutes late—like that's such a big deal. I'm here, and where's the tutor anyway? They could've started tutoring you—I can catch up."

"First of all, I'm the tutor," he said as my mouth dropped open.

I'd never met a fine tutor until I walked into room number 205, and I just knew the brown brother—in his early twenties, with a frame that showed me he worked out—could not be a tutor. No way.

"And if you could catch up, you wouldn't need to be in here anyway. This is one-on-one tutoring, not two-on-one. My time is very valuable."

All the attraction I had felt when I'd first walked through the door flew over my head. This dude was a jerk.

"All right, fine then, let's get to it. You're the one standing up," I said as I quickly plopped in a seat and opened my book.

"You're on the wrong chapter," he said, even though I was on the exact page we had been going over in class.

"This is what we did today."

"Yeah, but looking at your grades, we need to go back to the beginning of the book so you can clearly understand. It's like a building block—if the foundation isn't strong, everything else is going to crumble."

"Okay, whatever. Let's just start. How long is this thing going to be, anyway?"

"Trust me, I don't want to be in here any longer than we need to be. But I mean, really, you sort of need to lose the attitude."

"Me lose the attitude?" I said. "I just walked in, and you're getting all over me about a few little minutes of being late. You're acting like I'm not taking this seriously. I couldn't find the place, okay?"

"My number was on the tutoring form. See—right there. 'Cody Foxx. If any problems, please call.' There it is, right there. My cell didn't ring."

"I don't have a cell phone, okay, and I do need to pass this class. If you're here to help me do that, maybe we got off on the wrong foot."

"All right, cool. Let's start."

As much as I tried to resist liking the process, an hour into the session, we were already on chapter four, and I clearly understood the material. This Foxx had such a way of breaking it down and explaining. But then he went and "looked" at me. Most men look at me when they want to get with me. He was supposed to be teaching me something, and he was flirting.

"Uh, don't stare at me, stare at the book."

He squinted his eyes. "I don't understand. I'm waiting on you to respond. I just asked you a question. Now I need my answer."

Had I misjudged the glance? Did he have me so wrapped up that I was the one tripping? Not even hearing that he'd asked me a question? Okay, what was going on here? I didn't even know this guy, and my heart was slightly racing. I didn't like being out of control. I shouldn't forget that he was a smart mouth and an unpleasant worm.

"We've covered four chapters—that's enough for today," I said as I grabbed my book, trying to gather myself.

"Yeah, I guess it's time for us to go. What am I thinking? I can't give you extra time."

We both stood at the same time, and though he towered over me, we were close. It seemed like our bodies wanted to mingle, but that couldn't happen. He was the tutor; I was the student. No line could be crossed. So, without saying anything, we walked out of the classroom and went our separate ways. I took a deep breath, thinking, *What in the world was that all about? Wow.*

The nearby sister chapter was having a back-to-school jam. It was supposedly an annual affair for them. The girls in my Western Smith chapter were a little uneasy about going because they hadn't had any interaction with the sister chapter since the sister chapter had lost a member in the hazing car accident last semester. I was in the car with Hayden, Bea, and Sharon on our way to the jam.

"Penelope goes to school up here now," Hayden said. "Oh, Alyx, sorry—Penelope is our former chapter soror who got suspended for hazing us."

"She's in grad school here?" Sharon said.

"Yep."

"Wow, that's great," Bea said.

"She's supposed to be having some kind of preparty for us at her place," Hayden said.

"With drinks and stuff?" Bea said as she looked at me.

"I am not going to be all wild," I responded.

"Oh, we know you're not. You ain't drinking nothing," Bea joked. "Everyone else in the car is a senior—not you, Miss Margarita."

"Ha, ha, ha, ha, ha," I joked.

When we got to her place, there were Betas from the other school. Everyone gave hugs, and the sorors said they were still coping with the death of Rose from the car accident. They said they still missed her but were doing better. I hadn't gone through all that with them, so I felt left out. I found a couch and just sat.

Hearing words of their loss made me sad as I thought about my mom. Yeah, she was here now, but how would I feel when she was gone? Could I cope? Could I get through my pain? Could I keep on going?

Then this guy plopped down beside me. I could tell his larger body wasn't that of a female without even looking up.

"Why you looking so glum?" the husky voice said in my ear.

"Why do you care?" I said and then wanted to take back those words when I locked eyes with Cody Foxx.

"It's you," I said with excitement I couldn't explain.

"Yep, it's me."

Calming myself, I said, "I thought nerds didn't do anything but study. You're forty miles away from campus at a sorority party. What are you doing here?"

"What are *you* doing here?" he asked.

"I'm a Beta."

"I never would have thought that."

"Why? Because I'm Spanish?" I said as my neck rolled. "It isn't only an African American sorority, you know? Plus, I didn't pledge here."

"Oh, I didn't mean you shouldn't be a Beta because of your ethnicity. I meant because Betas get their work done, and you . . . well . . . need I say more?"

He was trying to make a joke, but he wasn't funny. I had a lot going on, and I thought for a second he would be a breath of fresh air. But maybe he wasn't all that different from all the other guys.

"I put my foot in my mouth big-time. I didn't mean to make you sad again. You're too cute to look gloomy," he said.

Butterflies flew in my belly. He'd just called me cute. But before I could even respond, Malloy walked into the place, came over, and grabbed me.

"I want you to meet everybody," she said.

I looked back at Cody, and he smiled. I tried to keep my eyes on him for some strange reason, but then one girl grabbed him. Then another soror started chatting with him, and the next thing I knew he was with the host, Penelope. I had to ask Malloy the scoop on them.

Malloy told me they supposedly used to date when she'd gone to Western Smith, and now they were sort of in the middle of trying to work out all that. Obviously Cody was older than I was, and he definitely thought I was underusing my talents. But there was something that intrigued me about him. As I was watching him, he was watching me.

Malloy saw where my eyes were focused. She hit me in the side and said, "Uh, I don't know what you're drooling over, but you can't have him. That's a soror's man. So don't even think about it."

"What? What are you talking about?" I said. "That's my tutor. I know him."

"And I can tell he wants to really, really get to know you. But, again, there will be none of that. That's a soror's man."

I didn't know Penelope, and, yeah, we were sorors, but I could convince myself that my relationship with Cody was a professional one. I told Malloy there was absolutely no way anything was going to happen between Cody and me. But then Cody came over to me and said, "You'll be on time tomorrow for our session, right? I really want to see you there."

I hung on his every word. I simply nodded, and he walked away. Malloy hit me harder in the ribs that time.

"I'm serious, Alyx. You cannot talk to him. Y'all got something going on; I clearly see it. I hope Penelope doesn't see it, because you talking to her man would be a serious breach."

GASP

Oh, I had to admit Malloy's boyfriend was fine. I was sitting in the stands at the New York Giants NFL game, which was a whole different world from my little Texas country one. Malloy was cheering on her man, and Torian and Loni were on the other side of her cheering on their feet, too. I was sitting down. I mean, I didn't know Kade. He had gotten us game tickets and flight tickets to come out there; plus, we were chilling at his place. I was a fan, but I was just relaxing. I was taking in the sights. I was at a pro game. It was so cool.

All of a sudden, the crowd screams died down, and a hush came over the crowd. Malloy screamed out, and Torian put her arm around her. Loni's face displayed sadness.

Without thinking, I said, "What the heck is wrong

with y'all? This is a football game. People fall down all the time."

Loni said, "Shut up! Quit being so insensitive. Her man is hurt, for real."

I could have slapped myself when I stood up, looked over the crowd, and saw number fifty laid out on the ground, not moving. I didn't know much about football, but I remembered my uncles and my brothers always saying when the trainers and folks from the sidelines came out with a stretcher, it was not good.

"I gotta go down there and see him. I gotta figure out what's going on. This is horrible. Oh, my God! He's not moving his legs!"

"He's gonna be okay," Torian said, holding her girl up.

How do you know? I thought, but I realized Torian had said that because she was trying to be there for her sister.

"Let's go. We're gonna go down there," I said.

Malloy panicked. "They're not gonna let me down there to see him. I don't have that kind of pass. He needs me. This is so bad."

"Yes, you do! You have the pass for after the game. That's enough to get someone to tell us something."

"I'm not his wife or anything like that," Malloy said as she walked to the aisle and tried to keep herself together.

"I'll go down there and take you," a lady behind us said in a worried tone.

She was white, and she had the biggest ring I'd ever seen in my life. She was decked from head to toe.

"I'm Karen, the quarterback's wife. You're Kade's girlfriend. He might need you right now. This looks pretty bad."

Malloy hugged Karen. Then we followed Karen up the stairs and then down a private elevator. Everyone knew who she was, and it was obvious why: her husband had it going on.

Malloy was a complete wreck, and Torian and Loni had her back, holding her up, rubbing her arms, telling her over and over it was going to be okay. When we got off the elevator, the lady said something to some guards, and the next thing we knew we were in a waiting area that looked pretty private and official while Karen was outside trying to get information.

"He worked so hard for this moment," Malloy said as tears dropped down her face. "People didn't wanna draft him because they said he was injury prone. He'd done so much to prove them wrong. All preseason he'd dominated, and now in the second game he goes completely down. How can I encourage him?"

Karen came in and over to Malloy. "He broke his ankle, and he's out for eight weeks. He's pretty devastated, but he wants to see you."

"I can't go in there," Malloy said, shaking. "I can't tell him it's all right. I know he's upset—"

"No, no, you can tell him," Torian said. "You can be strong. You can get him through this."

"Yes because his training's going to be crucial," Karen said. "A positive attitude will make all the difference."

Loni said, "And you know that's why you're here."

"I'm here for us to enjoy this weekend together after the game. Now we'll be at some hospital."

Torian said, "But you'll be there together."

I whispered, "And you're here because you support your man. Don't let him see you all down and out. Help lift him up. You can do this."

"Okay, okay, I can do this," Malloy said as she wiped her eyes and then left the room with Karen.

Torian and Loni just hugged each other like they were going through this as deeply as Malloy was. I could feel Malloy's pain. It was a surreal moment. I was in awe of their friendship. It was major.

Kade was all settled down in his apartment, and Malloy was content with taking care of him. Torian and Loni were okay with that, but I had come to New York to have a good time. Sitting around watching a football player recover wasn't my idea of fun.

"Why you sitting there looking so ticked?" Loni asked me.

Unable to be convincing, I said, "No reason."

"You wanna go out?" Torian said. "We are in the nicest apartment in New York, and you want to hit the town! Go on and admit it. We know you, girl."

"And if I did? What would be wrong with that?" I said as though I had to defend myself.

Malloy came out of her guy's bedroom and said, "Don't worry. Kade hooked it up." She dangled his car keys in front of us.

"What are you talking about?" I asked, completely confused. There was no way she could be trying to play hostess to us when she was playing nurse to Kade. "You're not gonna be able to leave to take us anywhere.

And as bad as I want to party, I wouldn't even ask you to."

"You do know New York though!" Torian added, licking her chops. "You've been up here all summer with your clothing internship and stuff."

"No, no, no. I'm not leaving."

"Well, I'm not going anywhere by myself. Thanks for his keys and stuff, but nuh-uh," Loni said, making me roll my eyes. I couldn't believe some of my sorors were such wimps.

"Where is the club? I can find it." I stood and went over to grab Kade's car keys.

"Uh, no," Malloy said, stepping in my way. All of a sudden the doorbell rang. "We got some fine gentlemen ready to take you guys out on the town."

"I'm not going out with strangers," Loni said.

I hit her in the side at the sight of the fine specimens who had come in and now stood in front of us. "C'mon, where's that adventurous spirit? And look at these guys. They are his teammates."

"Oh, teammates? Oh, yeah, yeah. I—I—that's fine. Yeah, give us a second. We gotta get ready," Loni said, completely changing her mind.

Torian and I just burst out laughing. Malloy knew how to do it. The three of us were all giddy as we talked about having a night on the town with some other Giants players. Unfortunately the camaraderie went out the window when we realized there weren't enough men for the three of us. What could we do with two brothers?

So I asked, "Where's the other one? In the bathroom? I

mean, there's three of us. One of us will be outnum-bered."

We all looked at Malloy, and she looked over at us like, *I'm sorry.* She said, "Ladies, this is Onyx." He was the tall one with wavy hair and muscles nearly ripping out of his form-fitting shirt.

I said, "You are the starting cornerback who got the interception and first touchdown today."

"Yeah, that's me. Who are you?" he said, looking me up and down, showing his tongue.

"These are my sorority sisters, Alyx, Torian, and Loni," Malloy said, pulling me back and allowing Onyx to check us all out.

However, the stud did not look at the two of them. His eyes did not move from me. All of a sudden the room got hot, and I could sense the hate.

"And this is TJ," Malloy said, introducing us to Kade's other teammate.

TJ was a light-skinned brother sporting the cutest little dreads. He had a very nice frame and was prettier than most women I knew.

He took my hand. "I didn't score a touchdown. Go on and say it."

"Yeah, but you're a fullback. You made some nice blocks out there." I took my hand back and gently rubbed his face.

TJ asked, "A football fan, huh?"

"Uh, it's not my favorite game, but my family loves it, so I guess some of what they like rubbed off on me."

"Darnell was supposed to come with us," Onyx said

as he stepped in front of TJ, "but it'll be just the two of us. Is that all right?" He held out his arm for me to put my arm through it. It was just an innocent little gesture, so I did.

"Oh, wait a minute, dawg. This one's for me," TJ teased as he tried tugging me away from Onyx. Before we'd even left the place, I had two new enemies in Loni and Torian, and as I walked out to the limousine, arm in arm with two hunks, I knew my sisters were behind me calling me everything unsisterly. But you know where they were saying it? Not to my face. I was ready to party. They could roll with it or be pissed all night. Their choice.

When we got to Top Flight, I took the party straight to the dance floor. Onyx, TJ, and I turned the place out. I didn't mind getting a little loud. I had two shots in the car, and I was loose. Shucks, all the tears and tension we'd had—making sure Kade was going to be okay—I was ready to unwind, and if Torian and Loni couldn't handle that, they should have stayed back at Kade's place.

"You guys are gonna have to dance with my girls!" I said to the two of them three songs later when I felt hands on the top of my body from Onyx and the lower part of my thighs from TJ.

TJ looked over at the dull chicks and said, "Your girls need to loosen up."

I rubbed his chest and said, "Well, maybe y'all can help them with that. For real, for real—do me a favor. Play with them."

"And if we play with them for a little while, you think we can get with you a little later?" Onyx asked, touching my neck.

" 'We'? Oh, you think I roll like that?" I backed away from them both, knowing they wanted to get kinky.

"I don't know. You seem like you know how to have fun."

"Where's the money for the drinks?"

"Why should we give you that? What's in it for us?"

"And to think Kade said y'all were gentlemen. Y'all tryin' to give me ultimatums and stuff. Don't you know if I wanted to get down like that later, I would? But if you gonna pressure me and stuff, we might as well end all the fun now."

"Oh, naw, naw. Here, here, we are gentlemen," Onyx said as he reached in his pocket and gave me a hundred.

"Go on over there and drink, and we'll dance with your girls for a second. Then we will be there to get you," TJ said. TJ was wearing a sports jacket. I reached over and put my hands where no one could see them, slid them down the back of his pants, and gripped his buns real tight. "Oh, see, now you playin'," he said.

"What? What? What she doing?" Onyx asked.

"Nothing I won't do to you," I leaned over and whispered to him as I let my tongue slide out to his ear. "Now go get my friends."

As the three of us walked over to Torian and Loni, they looked so mad. If looks could kill, I probably would have been six feet under.

"They want to dance with y'all," I said in a foul way.

I was trying to do them heifers a favor. I never needed

any help getting a guy, but I always had to help somebody else get lucky.

"The three of y'all seemed like y'all were doing just fine," Loni said coldly.

"Girl, you better get up out of that seat and go dance. You know you want to." I grabbed her arm, pulled it tight, and swung her into the arms of Onyx. I didn't have to say nothing to Torian. She was on her feet and quickly went over to TJ. I sat alone and ordered a couple more shots.

These two handsome Mexican dudes came over to me and sat on both sides of me. I said nothing, but I could tell they were eyeing me.

Finally one of them said, "We thought we'd never catch you alone. You know the black dudes can't really make you happy."

"And all these shots you drinking are not going to make you feel good," the other one said as he opened up his jacket a little, showing me some fun in a plastic bag. "We got a table right over there. You gonna join us?"

To keep the peace with my girls, I thought, *You know what? Why don't I just let them have those two fools?* I wasn't into anything crazy, I was simply messing with Onyx and TJ so they'd do what I wanted. To squash all that, I decided to hang out with my kind. I was trying a little something of everything.

Minutes later, after the drugs set in, my head started spinning, and my stomach started aching. Maybe it hadn't been the best decision to take drugs from strangers, but I wasn't happy here.

Torian and Loni came over to me. "We came to get our girl," I sort of thought I heard them say.

One of the Mexican guys said, "She's with us. She's fine."

"You don't even know where she lives or who she is. We came to get our girl." Loni grabbed my hand.

Onyx and TJ stood behind my girls. TJ said to my two guys, "We don't have no problem, do we?"

"We were just showing her a good time," one Mexican dude said.

Oynx said, "What the heck y'all been giving her, man?"

"I gotta go to the bathroom!" I shouted.

The one guy would not get up so I could leave. The next thing I knew, everything in me came up as I let out a long gasp.

PERTINENT

I woke up in silky sheets in a panic. I was sweating all over and replaying the night's events in my mind.

"You're okay, you're okay," I heard Malloy say as I felt a wet washcloth across my brow.

"Oh, my gosh, I feel sick. My stomach is burning," I said as I tossed and turned in the bed.

Malloy said, "You're going to be okay. You're going to be fine. Relax. Torian and Loni told me what happened. You're okay. You're at Kade's house now."

I needed some Tums or Pepto-Bismol or something to coat my stomach. I guess because I had been severely depressed about my mom and having my own pity party about my grades, I just kept doing one stupid thing after another. Now I had made myself physically ill.

"You're not supposed to be in here with me," I quietly uttered. "You need to be taking care of Kade."

"He's knocked out asleep. I heard you in here tossing. Torian and Loni were on duty earlier, but they're asleep now. I told them I would watch you. Kade would be so bummed if you got even worse overnight if somebody didn't watch you. He wanted to rush you to the hospital to get your stomach pumped for us to make absolutely sure all those drugs—or whatever it was you took—are completely out of your system."

"I know. Right. Urgh. What was I thinking, Malloy? I just hate myself right now."

"Well, first of all we need to get you a T-shirt." She walked over to a drawer and tossed me one of Kade's shirts.

It hit my nose. "It smells so good. You're so lucky to have a man so sweet."

"I just need to get him well, and I need to get my new friend well, too," she said as she handed me a glass of water.

"Drink this. Alyx, tell my why you did this, girl?"

"I don't know," I said, clutching my stomach. "I wish I had the answers." I looked away, rolled over on my knees, and held my stomach some more. I felt horrible, but Malloy wouldn't let up. She sat in a nearby chair, and ten minutes later when my stomach calmed down a bit, she asked again.

"Tell me, girl, what is going on with you? You know why you took something from some guys you didn't know? They might have been from Mexico like you, but so what?"

Torian and Loni have big mouths. Or maybe it was

good they cared. I had been tripping, and they hadn't left me alone.

Malloy got that I was ticked that they had talked. "Don't be upset. I wanted to know everything, so I made them spill the beans. And Kade was mad at his boys. They were supposed to be looking out for you, and they were trying to get in your pants. Then they turn you over to some strangers."

"I'm a grown woman," I said. "Kade isn't my dad."

"Obviously you're not big-girl enough," Malloy said. "Seriously though, Alyx, I know life doesn't seem fair, and you're dealing with a lot right now with your mom. Plus, I know you told me school and tutoring aren't working out all that well, but you got to shake it off and decide you want to make the right decisions. Maybe this turned out okay, but what if you had taken something you couldn't just throw up? None of us would have known what is was. Those guys bolted. None of us know how to get in touch with them or where they went. I guess I'm saying you've got another chance to get it right, but you've got to want to do right for you. Do you understand how crucial this is? This is your life, girl."

I reached over and hugged her. I really appreciated how much she cared, and in her embrace I felt the urgency. Someway, somehow I was going to shake off the silliness and get my life together.

A week later, we were back on campus in the Beta Gamma Pi sorority room we weren't supposed to still have. However, because our Chapter President's uncle was the president of Western Smith, he was allowing us to still use the space.

Though my chapter in Texas was smaller, we were big on parliamentary procedures. We used *Robert's Rules of Order;* this was the first thing we got trained in after we crossed. My past collegiate adviser believed in running an orderly meeting, but as I looked around the room at my line and Western Smith's line, I didn't even see Western Smith's collegiate adviser anywhere.

I sat there as the two lines started arguing about whether we should have a party and whether we should go around and help other chapters around with their lines. They were talking over each other. Then they starting saying some truly nasty stuff to each other.

Bea, in particular, said, "I know we're suspended, but having a little party to raise a little money isn't going to kill anybody. The National President isn't going to know everything we do unless somebody in this room has a direct line to her snitches."

"Oh, so what are you trying to say?" Malloy said with angry veins busting from her skull. "Because I want to do things right so we can get our chapter back in compliance and back on campus. I'm not letting some of y'all pull down this chapter again."

Hayden tried cutting in when her line sisters and Malloy's line sisters were almost at blows. "Everybody just needs to settle down."

However, sorors started screaming back and forth. The lines were ready to defend their point. Bea looked at me to join her side, knowing I had been hazed and may hold that against my line, and Malloy stared me down—she knew I truly felt bad about all her line had been through and that now I had second thoughts about hazing being right.

Actually, I didn't want to be a part of either group. They obviously needed some order, so I raised my hand. Everybody just stared at me and then quieted down for me to speak, but the chair didn't recognize me.

I motioned up front to Hayden. "Do I have the floor, Madam President?"

"Yeah, you may say something, Alyx."

"Well, I know you all are wondering why I didn't just shout out what I had to say, but you all aren't working in order. The chair has to recognize you before you can speak. I believe *Robert's Rules of Order* is an important book that keeps the feelings down and let's everybody be heard respectfully. Then you vote on what's best for the body."

"And how do you know all this?" Trisha asked impulsively, apparently having heard nothing I'd said about protocol.

Sweetly as I could, I said, "I wish you hadn't just talked out of turn, but to answer your question, my chapter got trained in it. That's one of the workshops we had to do—actually, we had to master it."

"Why is it even important?" Torian asked.

"Well, because you guys have been shouting at each other, and nobody is really hearing anyone's argument. As I sat here and listened, you all made good points, but if no side is really hearing what you have to say, it's ineffective for the chapter. *Robert's Rules* also says no one should speak on a motion more than twice."

"Motion? What's a motion?" Bea said.

"Well, that's just it. We've been discussing stuff, but there's been no formal way of placing that item out there for the chapter to officially discuss. To start this meeting, no kind of agenda was even adopted; thus, anything goes, and we're wasting time."

"Yeah, because I wanted to talk about some things, but the President didn't put it on the agenda. So we just had to go with what she wanted to talk about," Bea said.

"Well, that's because I'm the only one that takes the time to do the agenda," Hayden said. "I'm not saying it has to be this way."

"And that's why you are supposed to jot down the agenda in the beginning of a meeting anyway. That way, anybody can add or take away an item they feel we don't need to discuss. The agenda must be approved by a two-thirds vote. And if you don't even have a quorum present . . ."

"A quorum? What's that?" Trisha asked.

Malloy said, "The majority of your members present."

"I read the bylaws for this chapter, and we need two-thirds of our members present to do business. In other words, if two-thirds of the people are here, we can conduct business, voting, etc. If two-thirds aren't present, it's information only, meaning we can never vote on anything, and nothing can move out of this meeting."

"Wow, Soror Cruz. I am really impressed," Hayden said.

"I just want what's best for our chapter. When we fuss and argue and do all that stuff, people get all worked up, and we aren't working toward change. By operating within the confines of *Robert's Rules of Order*, I think we'll give the respect every soror here deserves and is looking for. Let the vote speak for itself. Our organization is based on moral standards, so whatever rules and grounds the National President sets, we have to stick by it, or we are jeopardizing this chapter. We could be suspended indefinitely, and I don't think anyone in this room would want to be accused of such an awful thing. What we do now affects those coming behind us; it's a high responsibility, and I know we'll all do what's right."

They looked at me, stood, and cheered. Wow. Maybe I did have worth.

"Act Now. Yeah, that's right. That's the title of this workshop," the sassy state director said to our chapter as we sat in the workshop for problem solving.

None of us were excited to be at the state round-up event in Bentonville, Arkansas. We all had to be there for many reasons: Malloy's mom had gotten our rooms comped, and there were no fees because we were suspended, and Grand Chapter had paid for it all because they wanted us to get trained. It was so hard being the only chapter kicked off campus—and we were the Alpha chapter, too. We were supposed to be the premier chapter. Though I was new to it all, I certainly knew everyone had high expectations of us. But we were a joke. Other collegiate chapters were talking about us, and we didn't like it.

The state director continued, "When you have problems in your chapter, everybody must take a good look at themselves. You may think your view is right. You might truly believe you got it going on. You might even think you have your chapter members' and chapter's best interests at heart, but when there is dissension, again, you have got to look within. That's my first point, ladies."

I looked around the room and saw a lot of my chapter sorors rolling their eyes—particularly Bea and Trisha. I didn't hang with them much anymore, but when I was new to the chapter, I had done a lot to lead them astray. As the trainer was telling us, I had to look within, too. Yes, it was college, and, yes, we should enjoy ourselves, but I didn't have to be so disruptive. And if I wanted to stay and make the chapter whole, I needed to get it together and keep it that way.

"Ladies, when we look at ourselves and our own weaknesses," the trainer continued, "when we don't take the criticisms of others negatively but rather look at how we can build from those criticisms and get better, we can get stronger. For example, if you're on a train track, and you see a big train coming toward you, do you stay there and get hit, or do you do something different to avoid the collision? Hopefully you get yourself off the train. Many of us think we can take on the thirty-cargo steel machine, and that's ludicrous. Beta Gamma Pi is bigger than any one person, but collectively it needs all of us to function; one person can make a hole in our great organization and begin our downfall. This particular workshop will help you work on fixing those holes, healing broken hearts, and finding resolutions so we can reach greatness."

I looked over at Hayden. She was a great leader. Not only was she taking notes, but she was smiling. She just had an upbeat personality, and it was contagious. As if reading my mind, our trainer said the next point was to look for the good in others.

"We always look at others and sometimes get jealous. That green-eyed monster comes out because of what they have and what we don't. Why not get behind their successes? Appreciate what you like in someone else, and use that to find positive attributes you like about yourself as well. Don't look at what someone else has and feel so threatened by it that you just wait for them to fail. That's not healthy. That's not sisterly. That's not what we need to do to move forward. If you concentrate on the good of your sorors more than you concentrate on the bad, Beta Gamma Pi will be stronger."

Malloy slipped me a note. *I love your presence.* I turned and smiled. Giving compliments was something I admired about her. She loved lifting people up. I probably needed to tell her that.

"Lastly now, ladies, to make sure we have the least amount of problems possible, seek to be peacemakers. Sometimes there will be beef between two ladies in your chapter, and you'll think, 'You know what, let me just stay out of the way.' Sometimes you'll have beef with someone, and you'll be like, 'Let me add fuel to the fire. Let me be the one who gets the last word.' No, no, no. If you look to find the good in your soror, look within yourself, and look to work it out—even if you had to pray your way through it—only then can we be the healthy organization we were meant to be. And, sorors, to get it right and truly right, you must do all this. You must act now. We can't afford any more problems. And as for the suspended chapter, everything I am saying is especially pertinent."

BICKER

I do not like him, I said to myself as I looked in the mirror in the bathroom, right down the hall from where I was about to have my next tutoring session with the fine Cody Foxx.

It'd been a while since any guy had lingered on my mind. There had been Tom Cruise, who I'd had affection for when I was in the sixth grade. Then there'd been Michael Kelly, the guy all the chicks at my high school in El Paso had liked, and as a sophomore in high school that senior had certainly caught my eye. But the real, real, real lovebug had never bitten me. Actually, I was too weirded out to think this could possibly be it.

As soon as I stepped into the hallway, I bumped right into him. During the awkward moment when our bodies touched, I knew there was something there my heart just couldn't control. I could tell he wanted to say something smart, but his lips stayed shut. His eyes devoured me, and I blushed. To keep from being off my cool game, I played like he didn't affect me.

I said, "So are we going to get this teaching thing started or what? You just going to stand there and stare?"

"Stare? You kidding? Shoot, I'm waiting on you. I know this stuff, remember? I'm waiting to see your alacrity," he joked, putting a sigh of relief out there for us to breathe.

"My what?"

"Your alacrity. A cheerful willingness or readiness to get the job done," he said effortlessly.

He needed to help me master English—that meant English papers. Not just writing, but rewriting, redrafting, and recomposing ideas, spelling, and not using the same word over and over again. I mean, it just was so much, and I knew I was lazy, but I had to ace this paper to bring my grade up to a respectable level. So every time Cody challenged me, I had to be ready to step up with alacrity.

After working for an hour, I said, "This is good enough. My professor will have to give me at least a ninety on this paper. All these new big words in here."

"But you need a hundred to bring your grade all the way up, and professors are objective. Why give him any reason to take anything off?"

Every time I gave a reason why what I had learned was enough, Cody came back, saying, "Come on, come on, come on, don't settle." My session was only supposed to be two hours, and we'd been there almost three. Something was making this guy stick around. He cared beyond his public-service duty or college credit.

"I want you to rewrite this paragraph. I'll be right back," he said, giving me space.

I needed to shake off the complacency, and the only thing I knew to do was sing. Sometimes when I got tired I'd hum a tune or two. I wasn't the world's greatest, and I wasn't going to cut a record or anything, but it relaxed me.

Aretha Franklin could hold it down. She was one of my mom's favorites, and *respect* just came out as I sat in the classroom. I was so into it. The paper in front of me was not what I was concentrating on. Mr. Too Stuffy, with his collar shirt buttoned all the way up to the top, came to mind even though he was nowhere in sight. He needed me to loosen him up some. Though I wasn't a virgin, it'd been a while since I had gotten my groove on. Yet the grad student was certainly making me think about it. So I sang, *"What you need, you know I got it."*

Then I was startled when he said, "You got it, huh?"

I almost crapped my pants. Seriously. I had been thinking of Cody, but I didn't want him to know it. I must have sounded like an idiot.

"Don't scare me like that," I said as I hit him across the chest.

"You've got a lovely voice."

"I do not. Quit saying that."

Pursing his lips, he said, "And the passion you sing with seems like you were singing about somebody."

"Don't even flatter yourself, Cody."

"I'm trying to give you a compliment. And I know

we've been bantering back and forth," he teased as he gently stroked my arm.

"Bantering?" I said.

"Yeah, the cute little play fussing we do," he said, stepping closer to me and taking my hand. "But I want you to believe me when I say your voice is mesmerizing. I wished you were singing about me."

I wanted to tell him, "I was. Now what?" But of course I looked away.

"I mess around on the keyboard a little, so tomorrow, if you're up for it, come by and let's mess around. I would be flattered."

"You'd be flattered, huh? Mess around, huh?" I blushed.

"Yes, I would be flattered if you dropped by." He grabbed my pen, tore a piece of paper out of my notebook, and added, "Come to this address."

Straining my eyes at the paper, I said, "I'm not going anywhere."

"Now don't fight me. Come to this address. You need extra sessions. I'm only signed up for a few. I'm giving you extra time. Do this for me. Dang, don't fight me on it." Cody was insistent.

Seeing his sincerity, I complied. "All right. You want me there, I'll be there."

We held a gaze so strong it felt like I could feel him breathing on my neck—and the fire was alluring. I knew we both felt something earth shattering.

The next day I checked and double-checked the piece of paper with his address as I stood in front of the theater on campus. Cody had said he messed around with the piano. However, there was a big audition sign for the upcoming play, *Know Love*, posted on the door.

What room is he in? I wondered. Did he expect me to find him? Giving him the benefit of the doubt, I walked into the half-packed auditorium.

The grand room seated nearly three thousand and was absolutely gorgeous. Historical-looking large columns with ornate pieces and velour seats an audience would be comfortable in amazed me. But I would never be good enough to perform there, and I knew Cody didn't intend that either. Where was he?

Then I looked around and saw there was no mistaking it: Cody was up on the stage. Not only was he playing the piano, he was giving direction to some girls who were trying to figure out how the song went. Clearly he was busy and absolutely was wrong to think I belonged in the same room where spring auditions were being held. I didn't want to just leave, because I did sort of want him to know that I had come by. Why I *really* wanted him to see me, I wasn't sure. As soon as he looked my way, five minutes later, I waved like, "Uh, I'm out, dude."

He got someone else to direct the play and jutted out into the hallway, following me. "Hey, Alyx, there you are. I was waiting on you."

"Well, I was standing outside for the longest time because you certainly didn't think I belonged in the theater, and I hope you don't think I'm—"

Cutting me off, he said, "Yes, I do. I know you should

try out for this play. I'm getting my master's in theater, and I know talent."

I wanted to ask him, "What, is it a part for a Spanish girl or something? You need me to speak another language and really hold your play down? Or you like my look or something? Don't try to use me or stroke my ego by telling me a lie." I knew I was no singer, and I wasn't going to let him tell me otherwise.

"Please, just come in for a second. Here's a copy of the music. Listen to the song. If you think you can sing it, try out for the part. Don't just walk out this door, though. You've got a talent you don't even know about. Trust me, it's rare that I hear raw talent as exceptional as yours. But you've got something. You were born with something special. You're supposed to use that gift. I would never steer you wrong. Trust me and try."

Okay, so he had me. I was a little intrigued. He had flattered me, and I did like all the sweet things he was saying about me. What was the big deal for me to sit there for a second and see if I could sing the song. If I felt like I wanted to get up, I could.

"Okay," I told him as he smiled and then led me back inside.

Honestly I sort of liked that he would owe me one either way this whole thing went. As I sat closer to the front, I was actually surprised when I saw Sharon, one of the Betas, take the stage. She was singing the same song he'd given me, and though the notes were nice, I wasn't really feeling them. She wasn't even really into what she was saying.

I knew the songwriter wanted more passion from the words. I looked closer to the top of the page and was stunned to see LYRICS AND MELODY WRITTEN BY CODY FOXX. He had real skills, and he needed someone to belt it out. So after she was done, he glanced my way, and I nodded my head. Next thing you knew, I was on the stage. I sang the heck out of that first verse. All kinds of *oohs* and *ahhs* were in the room.

However, when I went into the chorus, I suddenly sounded like a frog was in my throat. It was horrible. I hadn't heard that part played out, and I didn't have a clue what to do. When I looked to the side of the stage, Sharon was laughing. She was supposed to be my sorority sister, and there she stood, laughing. I let the microphone slide out of my hand; it made a loud, echoing thump throughout the auditorium.

Letting the street in me come out, I went over to Sharon, put my hand on my hip, pushed her back a little, and said, "Wait, what kind of sister are you? You standing here laughing at me?"

"Same kind of sister you are," she said as she shoved me back. "You're trying to audition for my role and really want to outdo me. This is a role I've been working for all summer. Now it's time for me to shine and for me to be the star during my senior year, and you want to come in here, some transfer, and steal my moment? I don't think so. Somebody needs to be real with you and tell you you're not African American, you're Spanish, and you think you can sing, but you can't, Miss White-Girl Wannabe."

Keeping my tough demeanor but feeling like tears wanted to break through, I looked over at Cody with a completely broken heart. I wasn't going to argue about it anymore. Sharon could have it all. I was through.

"Wait, wait, where are you going?" Cody said when I went back to the corridor.

I turned to him in tears and said, "You got to quit doing this. You got to stop following me. Go back in there to your sweet little play you created and leave me alone. I don't want to hear you tell me I can sing. I don't want to believe any of that mess. You heard me up there. I was horrible."

"No, I heard you try something you've never practiced. I heard you try something you've never heard, and you got it wrong—so what? When you sang what you had heard, you were the best of the day. No one goes onstage and jams it all the time. People have to be trained and coached—even your sorority sister. She's just intimidated. She wants the role by any means necessary. But she doesn't make the decision. She's not the director of this play. Come on, Alyx, you are stronger than that. Do not let a few little words keep you from shining. Plus, competition never hurt anyone. Make her work for it."

"I don't need to make her work for anything. I feel good about who I am, what I do, and what I have, and I've never been a singer. As Sharon said, I can't sing anyway, so stop pushing."

"Why should I stop pushing someone . . ."

"Someone what?" I said when he couldn't continue.

Suddenly Cody leaned over and kissed me. The moment

made me lose my breath. Gaining composure, I pushed him off me.

"Quit doing that. You're confusing me. You're mixing me all up. You're making me think . . ." I said, grabbing my head.

"Making you think what? That I'm acting?" Cody said, correctly guessing what I had meant.

"Yeah. Obviously you're pretty good at it, theater major, playwright, and love-song creator. You could say anything to make anybody believe whatever. Here I am, thinking you're some nerd, and you're practically Romeo. Please, I'm not the one."

"Okay, maybe the kiss was out of line, but I do care for you. Alyx, I wouldn't tell you you had talent if I didn't believe that. I want to give you the lead part because you shine more than anyone who has read the part. I want you to try. But you're right, it's not cool for me to mess up your head and make you think it's us and you singing or nothing at all."

"What is all this about anyway, Cody? Kissing me? Are you kidding?"

"I apologize, okay?" he said as he stepped back.

He was my tutor, for goodness' sake. He was a gradu-ate student. Why would he kiss me and confuse me like that?

"I can't stand guys sometimes. They know the right buttons to push. They know when a female is vulnerable. You guys overwhelm us like crazy, and then we fall for it and get our hearts broken. Well, I'm not going down that road. I'm not going to do this. Plus, you forgot I know you're dating another one of my sorority sisters."

"Penelope," he said.

"Yeah, yeah, Penelope. What about her? Where is she? How do you think she's going to feel if she finds out you're kissing me?"

"We tried things in undergrad when we were here. It didn't work out then. Yeah, she would like it to now, but I don't know. I had no intention in falling for . . ."

"For who? What, me . . . the dummy? Me . . . the Spanish girl? Me . . . the person you were saying can sing?"

"All of it. I just didn't know there would be a connection I couldn't dismiss. She isn't in my heart," Cody said as he looked away. Then he changed the subject. "Come back and try again."

"No, you don't understand. We do have a bond in our sorority, and sisterhood doesn't mean taking something away from somebody else. Not a theater part, and not a man."

"Yeah, but sisterhood also doesn't mean squashing people's talent, like Sharon was trying to do to yours. Or stopping true feelings, like I'm feeling for you."

"You don't feel anything for me. You're confused. Besides, I don't have any talent!" I screamed.

"Yeah, you do, and why do you feel so beat-down? Why do you feel like you aren't the bomb? Why do you think there's no way on Earth I could really be attracted to every part of you? You got a lot of stuff I don't know about and a lot of past pain I want to erase. I don't want tension with you. If nothing else, we've been real with each other. I believe you know I'd never tell you something I don't mean. Alyx Cruz, you're one heck of a woman."

Everything in me wanted to denounce all he said. So I huffed, turned around, and walked out the same confusing door I had walked in earlier. I wasn't going to hear any more of his lies. There was no more reason for us to fuss, and the only thing I could do to put distance between all I was feeling for him was to leave his presence and not bicker.

GOAL

"So you know no one should be alone for Thanksgiving. So you're coming home with me," Malloy said as she sat on my bed, trying to cheer me up.

Thanksgiving was a holiday I had always spent with my mom, and the thought of not being with her on possibly her last Turkey Day was hard to swallow. However, what could I do to get there? I didn't have a job or a man I could finagle to get me to Texas.

Truthfully a part of me didn't even want to be there. What was I going to run into? How would my mom look? Would she be too sick to even recognize me? How massive were her headaches? It just seemed better to wallow in my pity alone.

But when Malloy wouldn't leave, I said, "Really, I'm fine. You go have a good time with your family. I got everything I need here. Your dad has this place stacked, and with all the extra security he put in, you know I'm going to be okay."

"Uh, I'd thought you'd say that, so, here."

"What? I ain't taking no handouts," I said as my sister, roomie, and friend handed me an envelope.

It was a little thick. I couldn't see through it, but something was in there like money or a ticket, and I wasn't a charity case. I reluctantly opened it, and I was correct in my assumption of its contents.

"Can't take your money, girl. Seriously, Malloy, don't leave without taking this back." But of course she walked out, grabbed her suitcase, and then I heard the front door slam.

"Lord, why is my life so hard? You have given me the looks most have always thought were attractive. But I promise that everything else in my life seems cursed. When I just want to be angry and be all alone, you send me a friend like Malloy. Now I have the means to go see my mama. Even that may be too hard to bear."

A note fell to the ground. It read,

> *Alyx, my heart goes out to all you're going through, but, no, you don't have to go through any of it alone. I figured you wouldn't want to spend time with me and my family for Thanksgiving, because the only person you want to be with is your mom. Take this bus ticket and get yourself down to El Paso. Here's a hundred from Kade. He hates all you are going through and says he owes you for the bad time you had in New York. Not really—you did it to your-*

self—but he feels bad. I know you're laughing.
Give your mom a kiss from your roommate. Se-
riously you guys are in my prayers. —Malloy
    P.S. I packed you a bag in the closet. I'm out-
side right now waiting to take you to the bus
station, so come on.

Twelve hours later, I was in El Paso. I called my high
school buddy Pedro and he came and picked me up from
the bus station and got me home. When I stood in front
of our place, I cried. I didn't want to go inside my small
apartment and face my mom. I'd come all this way, and a
part of me didn't want to stick to the plan. But as the
wind blew, I felt a peace come over my heart, telling me it
was going to be okay, and without even using my key, the
door opened.

My mom called out, "Alyx, baby, is that you?"

"Yes, Mama, it's me."

I went inside and flung myself into her arms. All the
eeriness I had felt dissipated. Feeling her embrace was
comforting and safe. How could I have forgotten such
warmth? I didn't have great grades; I didn't have much
money. We didn't have much time, but we had much love.
We spent the rest of the evening catching up.

When I woke up the next morning I went into my
mom's room and lay down next to her and just listened
to her heartbeat. I couldn't imagine that sound not down
on Earth anymore. It was so steady, so soothing, and so
comforting.

"Alyx, you're moving around, sweetie. You okay? You
seem restless."

"Yes, Mama. I just don't know what I'm going to do without you."

"I'm here right now, and all we have is the moment. Let's seize the day. Let's make this one count. I've been cooped up in this house for weeks. Seeing you just gives me a burst of energy, like I've been outside running through the cherry-blossom fields."

"Oh, Mama, I don't know why you're saying that. I'm bringing you down."

"My dear, you could never bring me down."

"Mom, I don't apply myself well, and I want to make you proud."

"Well, if you want to make me proud, get it together and do it. Keep focused on what's in front of you. Always remember to take advantage of every opportunity. If you try your best and work your hardest, you'll always make me proud. And right here," she said as she pointed at my heart, "is where I'll always be. Don't lose sight of that."

We hugged, and that moment seemed to last. What a big blessing I had. My Thanksgiving was fuller than any turkey could have ever made me.

"You didn't have to come by and pick me up. I'm just here for a couple days," I said to my Texas line sister Sally.

"Girl, please, you're here, and we got a line you need to meet. And aren't you still trained to be with the pledges?"

"Yeah. We got trained in the spring, and certification lasts a whole year, so I can definitely see the pledges."

"Well, there you go. Booyah. You're able to work with

the Pis," Sally said, obviously excited about their thirteen pledges.

I had never taken over a line, because we'd just crossed last fall. But before I'd left school, we'd been trained in everything we needed to be able to conduct membership intake. That certification lasted for three hundred and sixty-five days, and though Alpha chapter wasn't able to have a line, my Kappa Upsilon chapter in El Paso was. Who knew when Beta Gamma Pi would be back on campus at Western Smith? There certainly was a possibility it wouldn't be before I graduated. So maybe this would be my only opportunity to get my hands into the pledge process. When I started thinking about it, I got fired up to go to one of the gem ceremonies.

"We already had two, you know," Sally said; she was the head of the line. "The Leadership Gem and the Sisterhood Gem ceremonies were well executed. All the Pis cried. Girl, us big sisters did as well."

"How'd they elect you Vice President?" I teased my buddy, knowing she had great leadership skills.

"Ha, ha, ha, you got jokes. I'm just so excited, and I have the heart to do this. We accepted every girl but one."

Curious, I asked, "Why didn't you let her on?"

"Well, because she had the minimum GPA," Sally said condescendingly, like a low GPA was horrible.

Offended, I said, "Okay, wait, I had the minimum GPA, and I got on line last year."

"Yeah, but you brought something different to the big sisters then," Sally said in a more accepting tone as she noticed my hurt feelings.

"What, because I was Spanish? Sally, I take offense to that. So the only reason they let me on was because I was different?"

"Well, I mean, yeah. At the time, you barely cut the mustard academically. Your ethnicity stood out. You didn't have much public service to show for yourself. You didn't have any extracurricular activities, like being in a sport or club or the arts. Girl, let's keep it real—you didn't even have a job to explain why your GPA was so pitiful. This girl this year was in the same boat, but she wasn't Spanish. She wasn't bringing anything to the table, so she needed to keep stepping. Beta Gamma Pi standards are a little higher than that," Sally said, sounding a little snooty.

I wanted to be mad. I wanted to be upset. But I couldn't argue with what she was saying. We did want the best. Why did it hurt me to know that I had barely made it and was still barely holding on? My GPA now wasn't even a 2.5, the minimum required to pledge. In one semester at El Paso, it had dropped as I had focused more on stepping than I had on the books.

There were five gem ceremonies the Pis had to go through. Because my old chapter had already had the first two, this one was on education, and maybe it wasn't by accident that I was attending it. The fourth gem ceremony would concentrate on Christian principles, and the fifth would delve into public service.

White candles adorned the nondenominational church's fellowship hall. The thirteen Pis walked in as we sang the Pi hymn. I could tell from their faces that they were so captivated by the moment. It reminded me how I had felt last year during the same educational ceremony. That one in particular truly moved me.

The new Chapter President, Megan Beverly, who I didn't really get along with because she always wanted to study while I was all about having a good time, was speaking to the pledges. "I vow to give my all, to learn as much as I can, to be better than I was yesterday. Although it may be hard for me to rise, I will take in the warm water going over my body. May it cleanse my spirit and make me renewed, ready, and able to strive for excellence and never settle for less. If there is a time that I don't devour my education and I'm not maximizing the knowledge, help me see the error of my ways so that I can get it right and become all a Beta is supposed to be."

Taking the gem ceremony into my heart was like a rebirth. I felt revived and inspired to be better than I was.

A couple days later, I was back at Western Smith, and though I'd had a great trip and felt like I was ready to conquer the world and finally get it all together, I was broken again when I opened a letter from the dean. I had less than two hours to be in the president's office to go over my status as a student.

"Malloy!" I yelled out.

"Hey, girl, you're back."

"Yeah, the bus got me back to campus."

"You know I would've picked you up. That's still a few miles' walk."

"You did so much. Plus, there was another college student who lives this way on the bus, so I just grabbed a ride."

"But you didn't know that person. You can't take rides from strangers, girl. The lady that lived next door to me all last year was crazy."

I joked, "I know. That's why you did a full background check on me before you let me in here."

"How'd you know about that?" Malloy teased back. "For real, I don't want to find you on the side of the street. Please call me next time. I was worried, for real. I'm here for you. Dang, why is it hard for you to accept help?"

"Okay, I hear you saying that. Well, I need some help right now."

"What? Name it. Your mom all right?"

"Yeah, she is as well as can be expected. I went to the third gem ceremony back home, and it was awesome."

"Really? Are you allowed to do that? We're suspended."

"Alpha chapter is suspended, but I was down there with Kappa Upsilon, and we're still on the yard. I could be with them because I've been trained."

"Oh, go, girl. Gem ceremony three is major. The education one where you're showered in warm water is so refreshing. Though at the time I wasn't ready when they poured that warm water on me."

"I know, right."

"What do you need?"

"Look at this." I handed Malloy the letter I badly wanted to burn with a match.

"What do you want me to do? This is from our college president. I don't know him like that."

"Yeah, but you know Hayden really well. Isn't this her uncle?"

"But he's not going to help us. Our chapter is kicked off the yard, so you know he won't pull any special favors. You're just going to have to buckle down and get the right grades. They're talking about probationary terms; they're not saying they're going to kick you out today. You got a chance, but you got to face the music. You just left gem number three—you should be fully charged to do this."

"I am, I am, but, I mean, I'm not A-student material."

"You don't know what they're going to tell you. You might not need As but you're cutting yourself short. I believe in you more than you believe in yourself, Alyx, and I don't understand why. You can make any grade you want to make, including As."

"No, I can't. I don't know if I'm dyslexic or just have some kind of other disability nobody's figured out yet, but learning just doesn't come easy to me."

"Okay, so you got to study a little harder. We can work this out, but you got to be willing to try. Come on, I'm heading to class."

"I got to shower."

"Uh, you got to get to a meeting, and I don't think you are in a position to be late. Let's go."

I grabbed my purse and book and left with Malloy. She gave more encouraging words as we got to the president's office. She actually walked in with me and said something nice to Malloy's uncle. He smiled my way, but I knew the facts were the facts. I sure appreciated her trying though.

"So you're back again? You're doing better," the dean said after all the introductions and I was seated. "But you are still not completely off academic probation. We take value in our minority scholarships, and while we're extremely excited to have you here, Alyx Cruz, you've got to find your way. You must put in the effort, and you really have to turn this GPA around. You came here with a two-point-two. With summer class, you had a two-point-four. Looking at your grades for this fall semester, now you're around a two-point-six. By the spring semester, you need to have a three-point-oh. So, exams are coming up, and you need to close it out with a bang. How's the tutor working out for you? He rarely gives people great remarks, but he's been saying you're a hard worker. Do you feel he's helping, or would you rather do it on your own?"

A lump came to my throat. I hadn't thought about Cody in days, but as soon as there was a mention of him, my heart skipped a beat. "No, no, no. I like the program you guys have set up and placed for me." I stood. "And I promise I won't let you down. I'm going to get a three-point-oh this semester and next semester. I want to be at Western Smith College. I'm not going to take my eye off the goal."

PIERCED

I went in for my next tutoring session and found a note from Cody. I was shocked when I read it.

Alyx, I thought long and hard about it, and I'm just not going to be able to tutor you anymore. I really think you're great and all, and clearly I have upset you by not being absolutely forthright about why I wanted you to come to the theater. I know you're fine academically. You've proven that as hard you've worked these last few months, you can soar academically. I'll see you around.

C

"What the heck is this?" I said, pacing back and forth, rereading his note for the tenth time as if reading it again would change its message.

When it sank in that he was ditching me, I dropped into the chair. Yeah, I had worked hard, and I wasn't saying Cody was my only motivation factor, but he was such a great coach. He knew how to make me not only understand the material but *want* to get it. I knew I couldn't get a 3.0 or better without him on my team.

When I thought back to a week ago when we'd had our rough conversation and I'd basically just left, telling him to get out of my face, I knew I had to make things right. I had to let him know I wasn't angry with him. He had to go forward with the tutoring.

I didn't have his home address, but I did have his number. When I called, I got his machine. It didn't take me long to think where he could be. I went back over to the theater, this time up to the balcony, and waited until his rehearsal was over. Clearly he was frustrated by the cast, but I was frustrated that he'd walked out on me. I didn't know if this was a good time or not, but we had to work this out. He had to know I needed his help. So, after practice, I caught up to him.

"Uh, can we talk for a second?"

I could tell when his eyes widened that he was shocked to see me. He looked away, but that didn't deter me.

"Seriously, I need to talk to you."

"I think I said everything in that letter, Alyx. If this is about me tutoring you, there's no need for us to chat. I just think it's best you leave it alone."

Everybody was looking at me—folks I didn't know, they looked all concerned, like, "What's she going to say next? Is he going to help her? Oh, the drama continues."

But this wasn't a play, this was my life. Cody needed to help me. I wasn't here to entertain his cast and crew.

So I walked closer to him and whispered, "Alone, please. Now."

Then I strutted away, shaking my hips to the left and right. I used what I had to make the dude drop everything and follow me immediately. I knew I was successful when I heard the rumblings of others followed by footsteps behind me. Yeah, he was coming. I could do this. I could talk to him. He had to see I needed his help.

"It's private right here. Let's talk!" he called out.

Turning around, I said, "Okay, so you're just sending me a cold note dropping me. That was pretty cruel."

"What are you talking about? It's not like we're cool. You made that pretty clear last week. And the note wasn't rude."

"I know, but I was caught off guard with this whole being-in-a-play thing. I mean, you signed up to be my tutor. I meet with the president of the school and the dean, and thanks to you—"

"No, no, no, thanks to all the hard work *you* did. I just told them the truth. You deserve to keep your scholarship so they get behind you. You know I've helped you fly. Now it's your turn to soar."

"Well, I just don't think I can rise without your help," I said as I moved even closer to him.

"Well, you're going to have to because I can't. I just think we're too close, and you don't need all that. It's not going to work." He turned and walked back toward the stage.

Watching him move farther and farther away, my heart sank. Something in me wanted to be connected to this guy. Maybe I had messed up that chance for good.

"Wait a minute, wait a minute. Please come back. What is it I can do or say to make you help me? Cody, please."

All of a sudden, the fine specimen in front of me stopped walking. I didn't know what to do or how to respond. I didn't want to push him too much, and I'd already begged sincerely. When he didn't turn back my way, I realized there was no hope and that somehow I had to find a way to make it without him. Whatever I thought I was feeling for him, I needed to let it go.

Just as I gave up hope and turned to exit the building, he called out, "Alyx, come here. I got something you can do to help me, and then I'll help you."

"You want me to be in this play that badly?" I said as I walked back to him, knowing that was what he wanted.

"Yeah. You have an amazing talent."

"You saw me sing that last song."

"You didn't know it. Let me train you. This is what I'm studying. I'm not saying I'm going to be a big Broadway director one day, but that is my dream. I know this game. I know what can move a crowd, and not only are you beautiful, but you've got an amazing presence that will capture an audience and really bring home the message of this play. Alyx, I think you just haven't tapped into your passion. You wonder why you're average in your studies and why you don't have that excitement to keep pushing sometimes unless you got a cheerleader by your side rooting you on like I have been these last couple of months. But for you to be self-motivated—for you to be passionate, you've got to want it. You've got to dream about being something. You've got to have a desire to learn any and everything about it so you can succeed."

"And you're telling me you think acting is it?"

"I can't say for certain," he said, taking my hands into his sweaty palms, revealing his nervousness. "But I got a good hunch on this. I mean, you ain't feeling nothing for anything else you're doing. You don't want to be a teacher; you don't think business is it. Why not give acting a try? Why not see if this is your thing?"

When he said that, it hit something inside me, something deep, something real. Something that made me think, *I don't want to miss out on what my calling is in this world. I don't just want a paycheck.* I did not have any type of love or desire for anything special in my life careerwise. He was right—what did I have to lose?

"Okay, I'm in."

When he threw his big, strong, warm arms around me, it felt too good. Memories of his kiss flooded my thoughts.

Breaking my trance, he said, "I got a couple more hours of practice, and I want to give you the script and introduce you to the cast. Then we'll go study for your exams. Cool?"

"Yeah, cool," I said as we pulled away from each other. Something in the way he looked at me gave me a tingling feeling all over. I exhaled, thinking maybe my life was finally turning around.

*   *   *

The next day I was studying my lines at home when I got a knock on the door. Malloy always played hostess, but she wasn't home. So I went to the door, and there stood Sharon on the other side of the glass. Her lips were pouting, and her hand was on her hip like I owed her something. I did not have time to get into a whole bunch of drama with her. I turned around to walk back into my room. She kept ringing the doorbell annoyingly.

So, despite my better judgment, I turned back around, opened up the door, and said, "Yeah, what?"

"Oh, that's how you greet somebody?"

"Girl, look at how you're standing. Like you're mad before I even say hello. Let's not front and pretend there's no tension between us. You're mad I've got your role in the big campus play. You're ticked about it."

"I just can't believe you accepted it. This is your first time. I'm a theater major. This is a big deal to me. Alyx, you could care less about this whole thing. You're only interested because you think Cody is cute. You know he's one of our soror's men in the first place? Shows you don't care anything about loyalty. Screw Penelope, screw me."

"Wait a minute, you don't have to talk to me all crazy," I said to her. "I'm giving you the courtesy of listening to whatever it is you came over here to say, but you need to do it with some respect."

"Like you respected me with my part you just snatched away?"

"I didn't snatch anything away. I'm not the director. I've got no pull. As you said, this whole world is new to me, but the man has a vision of what he's trying to do, and it's none of your business what I think about him. Just because I'm new here, it doesn't mean I don't know anything about you. Remember who I live with. Weren't you trying to take somebody else's man yourself?"

"If you're referring to Kade, you don't have it right. He was my boyfriend first."

"Whatever. From what I heard, Kade was not interested in you for the longest time, and you kept holding on to nothing. But you know what, I don't even know why I'm going there with you."

"Yeah, I don't even know why I thought I could come over here and talk sense into you."

"What, you just thought I was going to give up the part?"

"Why can't you try to be my sister and help me get it, help me learn it, help me act it, help me understand what this whole thing is supposed to be about?"

"Sharon, if it's about the sisterhood, and if it's not just about you or me, why can't we go with what the director decides?"

"Because all he's thinking with is his pants. He's not really looking for the one with the skills," she said, insinuating that I had given it up to get the part. "I've studied theater for eight years. That's all I've ever dreamed of doing and being. And here you come, some amateur. This isn't supposed to be this way."

"But he gave you the next biggest role. Can't you maximize that?"

"Why don't you take that role, if it doesn't seem so bad, missy, huh?"

"Okay, Sharon. Please leave. Let's agree to disagree."

The telephone rang, and I was so excited to grab it. The last thing I wanted was to continue arguing with her. Hopefully she would see herself out, but she just stood there.

It was Pedro, my homebody from El Paso. "What's going on?"

"Everybody here is shaken up, so they asked me to call you." In a dismal voice, he said, "It's not good, Alyx. It's not good at all."

"Why? What do you mean?" I asked, but then remembered I had no other real family in the U.S.

Malloy came in through the front door, and I could hear Sharon pleading her case. "You told her I tried to take Kade?"

"That is not even what I said," I said to Malloy as she came my way.

I was just so frustrated, but then Pedro spoke again. "This is serious, would you listen, please?"

"I'm sorry. I'm just dealing with drama with my sorority sister."

"It's your mom."

"My mom?" I gasped. Sharon and Malloy stopped fussing.

"She passed away this morning."

"Huh?" I said as I slumped down in the nearby chair.

"I'm sorry, Alyx."

"My mom is gone!" I cried out.

All of a sudden, being in a play didn't matter at all. I

just dropped the phone. Malloy took it and started talking to Pedro. Sharon, as distant as we were, put her arms around me, and even with the sincere comfort she was giving me, knowing that my mom had left this world meant my heart was forever broken and pierced.

10

BROKEN

At that point, I wasn't a twenty-year-old woman anymore. Instead I was a pitiful little baby curled up in a fetal position. The only problem was I did not have a mom to cradle me and tell me it was going to be all better.

Giving credit where credit was due, I will say that Sharon and Malloy tried hard. Minutes went by, and I still kept crying. Hours went by, and the pain wouldn't go away. Before I knew it, it was dark, and they both were still there telling me it was going to be okay. If this would've been my apartment, I would've broken something. If I'd had one more chance to be with my mom, I would have told her, "You can't die, you got to stay alive for me." No matter what I'd done, no matter what I didn't do right, my mom had still cared, and she'd told me I had a purpose.

Without her presence, without her love, why should I have continued to have faith?

"I'm just coming in to check on you," Malloy said.

I looked over at the clock and saw it was eleven. I couldn't say, "I'm okay." I wasn't, but I didn't need her worried. She had acted better than any friend I'd ever have.

"I'm still here, too," Sharon said, peering over Malloy's shoulder.

"Hey, y'all, don't sweat. I'm cool," I lied confidently.

Sharon looked in my eyes. "You are a much better actress than I thought. We're going to get through all this together."

"No, no, I'm not acting. I'm serious. I'm okay," I said, widening my eyes so they could see no tears.

"You're not okay. You need us to get something or someone? You want the rest of the sorors? Whatever you need, you tell us, and we're ready to do it," Sharon said, being overly sweet.

"You know what, Malloy, can I just borrow your keys for a while? I just want to go for a drive by myself," I said as Sharon looked at her like, "Uh, that's not a good idea."

Malloy looked back at me. "I can take you wherever you want to go."

"But that's just the point. I sort of want to be alone."

"It's late."

"I just need time to think. Please? I won't be gone long." I could tell the two of them were hesitant. I had no idea where I was going to go. I just knew I needed to get out of this stuffy place and scream. I got up before Malloy had even said yes and put on some tennis shoes. I grabbed my Beta Gamma Pi jacket and was out.

Malloy said, "Yeah, I'm sorry, Alyx, I just don't think this is a good idea. Let us watch over you. Stay here tonight. Take the car tomorrow."

"Listen, I don't want to seem ungrateful, but you just asked if there was anything you could do for me—name it and you'd do it. All I want to do is take the car for a little drive, clear my head, and come back. What is the big deal? There's no need to act like my mom, okay? My mom is gone."

"Okay, okay, I got it. Here, here are the keys. Be careful," Malloy said.

I couldn't even say thank you, I was so upset. I grabbed them, got into her brand-new convertible Ford Mustang, looked in my pocket, saw that I had a twenty-dollar bill, and headed straight to the liquor store. I found my fake ID and bought a bottle.

I went to the empty parking lot at the school theater, opened up the bottle, and chugged it in the car. It was nasty, but as the warm drink hit my uneasy spirit, all of a sudden I felt calm, numb, and anything but sober. For that, I was grateful.

I had to be the biggest idiot in the world, sitting in the crowded parking lot with tons of campus police all around while the liquor bottle was in sight. But I guess consequences didn't really matter to me at that moment. My mom was gone forever, and I felt all alone.

Then I saw Cody coming out of the theater. A girl wearing a Beta Gamma Pi jacket was with him, and though I didn't have all my faculties, I could tell it had to be Penelope. She was all up on him. If memory served me correctly, he had told me in the theater foyer that he was done with Miss Penelope.

"Dang, why don't y'all just get with each other right in the middle of the street?" I yelled out, but they couldn't hear me because my windows were up, thankfully.

I drank more and more and became a basket case, watching them. I tried hard to focus on something other than Cody and Penelope, but I was all entranced, watching them carry on back and forth with each other as if they were in a soap opera.

"Can't you see the boy doesn't want to be bothered with you?" I yelled out again as I saw Cody walk away from Penelope.

Penelope went galloping behind him. Then, like she was some stray dog, he tried shooing her away. The problem was she wasn't a stray. They'd had a relationship, and I could see they were on their way to reconciling.

When some of the other Betas came out of the theater and took Penelope inside, Cody got in his car to leave. This was my moment, so I cranked up Malloy's engine.

He later pulled into his apartment complex, and before he walked inside, I raced out of Malloy's car and snuck up behind him.

"Hey," I said, my breath reeking.

"Hey," he said in a startled tone as he stepped up close to his apartment door.

"It's me, Cody. Can you let me in? I just want to talk to you. I just want to be with you, you know? Hey. I saw you with Penelope. Y'all are through. Obviously you didn't want to be with her because you want to be with me. Well, I'm ready," I said, falling into his arms.

He caught me. "What are you doing?"

"I just want us to have a little fun," I said as I went straight to rubbing his waist.

"Okay, what's going on? Alyx, this isn't like you."

"Why do you care?" I huffed, giving him a big whiff.

"Okay, you need to come in right now because obviously you've been drinking."

"So what—I've been drinking. So what—I've been having a little fun. I feel good, and I'm trying to make you feel that way, okay?" I said as I wobbled into his place.

It was a cozy one-bedroom loft. Not new, not completely neat, but not a total mess either. I looked around and scouted out his bedroom.

"Okay, so I'm going to go in here and get undressed," I said as I lifted my shirt.

"Wait, no, no, no, no, no. You just sit here while I make you some coffee."

"What? You don't want to get with this?" I said, pointing to myself.

"What I want you to do is tell me what's wrong. I'm going to jump in the shower real quick because I'm sweaty from the theater party, and then we can talk, okay?"

I leaped into his arms and placed my lips on his.

"What are you doing?" he said as he shoved me back. "Let's talk, okay?"

"Fine, go take your little shower then," I uttered in a ticked-off tone.

"It'll be just one second. I'm going to brew this coffee

as soon as I get out. You drink my strong brew, and we can talk."

I looked away, and as soon as he went into the bathroom, I grabbed Malloy's keys and was gone. Though he had not kicked me out, it felt like he had kicked me in the gut. I couldn't take any more letdowns, and my buzz was wearing off. So as soon as I got in the ride, I drank whatever was left of the liquor, hoping once again it would make me feel better.

I couldn't get out of the parking lot fast enough when I saw Cody standing at his door in a towel, drenched, trying to tell me to stop. What was the big deal? I knew how to drink and drive, though I didn't have a car of my own. I wasn't that out of it—just needed a little something to take the edge off all the pain I was feeling.

Thinking about my mom and knowing I would never see her again was just more than I could take. And when the bottle fell out of my lap, like an idiot, I reached down, forgetting I was on the highway, and zigzagged, running another car off the road.

My heart raced, I was scared so bad seeing the bright lights coming toward me. Though I felt as though I didn't want to live, the last thing I wanted to do was take someone else's life. What was I doing? What was I thinking? Why was my life such a mess? Quickly I got out of my car and ran over to the car I had made swerve. I clutched my heart when I saw a lady with a baby in the backseat. I just fell to the ground.

"Oh, God, what did I do? Oh, no, God, help!" I cried after seeing the airbag, fully engaged, and the baby crying at the top of its lungs.

Frantically I tried to open the door, but it was locked. I just kept trying, praying it would open. Nothing was right.

"Say something! Say something!" I banged on the window. The lady's eyes opened, and I was relieved. She unlocked the door, and I opened it.

"My baby," she said in a weak voice.

"The baby's crying. The baby's okay," I said.

"Oh, my God, you were drinking. You could have killed me and my baby. Oh, my gosh," the lady accused when she smelled my breath.

I couldn't stop her tears, and I couldn't stop them from my eyes either. It was an absolute mess, and then red and blue lights started flashing—two sets of them. And before I knew it, I was breathing into a bag and trying to walk a straight line.

"Take me to jail. I don't deserve to live. I could have killed a baby," I said, obviously really out of it as the stars were spinning around me. "Why didn't you want me?" I said to the police officer. He looked like Cody.

"Ma'am, I don't know who you think I am, but I'm an officer of the law, and I'm placing you under arrest for driving under the influence."

I shook my head and then clearly saw that the white gentleman was not Cody at all. The lady I had almost hit was screaming. She was very angry.

When the officer stepped away to talk to the ambulance driver, I went over to her and said, "You know, my mom died tonight, and I am so sorry for this. I hate myself for endangering you."

As I started crying I noticed Cody's car was pulling up.

He came running out straight toward me. How could I face him after all I'd done?

"What's going on, Alyx? You all right?"

"Sir, you have to step back. I'm taking her in for a DUI. She almost hit a woman with a baby in the car this evening. If she doesn't have an attorney, I suggest you get one for her or get her bail."

"I'm sorry," Cody said to me. "I called your roommate to see if you went home. She told me everything about your mom."

I just looked up at the sky with tears streaming down my face. It wasn't Cody's fault. He'd tried to give me coffee to settle me down. It wasn't the officers' fault. They were just doing their jobs. They had no choice but to take me in for breaking the law. It wasn't Malloy's fault. She'd just been trying to appease me and allow me to get some air. It was my fault, and mine alone. I was so confused and hurt. As I got into the police car, with no mom and no freedom, I'd never been more broken.

11

GESTURE

"You go to Western Smith, girl? What you do to get locked up in jail?" asked some lady I was sharing a jail cell with.

The lady looked like a streetwalker, and she kept staring boldly at me. I just wanted to be left alone. The reality of being in jail for a DUI and nearly causing a accident that could have killed people was weighing heavily on my heart.

"Okay, I'm just trying to talk to you, I'm just trying to be nice. We gotta be in this cell together, so the least you could do is give me some respect. Just 'cause I ain't no college girl don't mean you any better than me. You better act like you know we in the same boat right now, Ms. Goody Two-Shoes."

I wanted to ask her how she knew I went to Western Smith, but then I realized my BGP jacket had the school's patch on it. I wasn't looking down on her. I just wanted space.

"I'm sorry. I'm not trying to be rude or anything like that. I just need to think, okay?" I replied.

"Well, you gonna have a lot of time to think. It's late, and you probably ain't going nowhere tonight. You're gonna be here till morning, girl."

Finally the lady walked away and sat on the bunk across from me. I was happy she could tell I was distraught and needed time to myself. However, five minutes of silence was all she gave me. She started in with more questions.

"For real, I'm curious—what did you do? A good-looking college girl like yourself with all your hopes and dreams right in front of you, you don't have to sell yourself on the streets like me. I hope you weren't trying to do that, especially not wearing those baggy jeans and that big-old oversize jacket." She flared her nose and then modeled around our cell. "You gotta show some skin, you know what I'm saying?"

I couldn't help but laugh watching her walk around our small space. Then I realized she was trying to make me laugh. It had worked.

"I had way too much to drink, and I was behind the wheel," I opened up and said.

"Ooooo, you know that's a big charge?"

Feeling a headache coming on, I said, "Yeah, now I do." I put my hand over my head and leaned against the bed rails. Had my horrible actions gotten me some type of permanent record? Would I be able to get out of here?

"Listen, people make mistakes all the time," she said when she saw I was feeling bad. "You'll get out of here.

It's your first time. You make up some kind of good excuse with the judge, and they might suspend your license, but they might not even put it on your record if you go to class. You'll be okay." She had a comforting voice. "But when you get another chance, when you get back out there and go to them classes and stuff, think about Ms. Sally here. I need you to do good for folks like me who have thrown so much away."

I had wanted to be left alone. However, God had sent her to help me know that all was not lost. I still had an opportunity to make things right.

I moved closer to her and listened as she continued. "Here I sit, having dropped out of school in the eleventh grade. Never got my GED. Because all the guys told me I was fine, and I saw my mama making a living selling her body, I thought that was the best way to go. Little did I know going to college and getting a better education would be the only thing that would get me a real chance in this world. Girl, you have that chance. Do something with it other than drink yourself into jail."

All of a sudden, through the pain of a pounding head, it was so clear to me. Everything Ms. Sally was saying made such sense. Just her taking the time to be real with me and honestly telling me she wished she could be in my shoes allowed me to get a message from the Lord.

"Thanks, Ms. Sally, you just don't know how much I needed to hear that."

"Well, don't just hear it, girl, make sure you heed to it," she said as we heard footsteps coming down the hall. "Betcha they coming to get you right now."

When I looked up, there was a guard standing before

us. "Young lady, a bailsman has posted the funds needed for your dismissal."

Though I didn't know Ms. Sally, and we came from completely different worlds, she had taken the time to share a word of encouragement with me at my lowest point. I had to hug her. And in that embrace, I felt my mom saying, "Make sure you get it. You need to do better for this lady, for me, and for all those out there who have a dream that wasn't pursued because we didn't take our education seriously."

"You be good now," she said, letting me go.

"Yes, ma'am, I will."

When I went back to the booking room, I was greeted by an older man who looked just like her, Malloy, and Cody. My eyes became heavy with water again. I didn't deserve such support, and I was humbled by it.

The older gentleman carrying a briefcase said, "Hello, Alyx. I'm Malloy's father. My daughter cares a lot about you and told me your story. I identify with what you're going through, so I came to help by posting your bond. You do have a hearing next month, but due to the extenuating circumstances of your mother's untimely death, you are going to be released now on your own recognizance. Even though you are not supposed to be going out of the state of Arkansas, your tutor, Mr. Cody, has permission to drive you down to Texas to take care of your mother's affairs. He will assure you get there safely."

I couldn't even look at Malloy, knowing that she had trusted me with her car and here I was in jail having driven under the influence. Her car was brand-new. I had truly let her down. It was so moving, though, when I didn't have to say anything—she just came over and grabbed my hand with the largest smile on her face.

"It's all good," she said. "I had to get my dad to help. We need each other and I thank you for being there for me this year. Honestly, after my stalker incident last year I would have been scared living alone."

Fighting back still more tears, I walked out hand in hand with my true friend.

Then it dawned on me again that Cody was nearby. I didn't know what to say to him either. For him to take the time to come and then go out of his way during the holidays to drive me more than eight hours to El Paso was overwhelming.

When we got outside of the precinct, Mr. Murray said, "I do see young people really turning their lives around. You're at a crossroads right now. You can beat the odds. Though you're down, you don't have to stay that way. I challenge you. Excel for your mom. Excel for the people who care about you. Most of all, excel because you can."

"Yes, I will," I said, extremely thankful that I'd been to the bottom and had come out of it all right.

"I lost my father when I was ten," he said to me. "Growing up without a dad definitely wasn't easy. I had a lot of people say I wouldn't become anything because of it. But I kept his legacy in my heart, and that propelled me to strive for my best every day. Now, Miss Cruz, you can do the same thing. With today's opportunities you can achieve more than I have."

"Thank you again. I won't let the school down again."

"Good," Mr. Murray said before he left the precinct.

"Cody, I don't have to go my mom's service. It's probably really not gonna be a service anyway," I said as we approached his car.

"It's okay, I'll take you," he said. "You need to say good-bye. I'll be there for whatever you need."

"I don't have any clothes or anything," I said, just wanting to get in bed and stay there.

Malloy pointed into his backseat and said, "Yeah, you do. I packed a couple of your things and even bought you a few new ones. Your suitcase is already in the car."

"You didn't have to do that, you've already helped me so much. I let you down—I mean, I almost wrecked your car."

"But I prayed for you, and you didn't wreck anything. God kept you safe. Last year some of my friends helped me go to Kade's football NFL tryout. Now it's my time to return the favor and help someone else."

Malloy and I hugged. She told me the cops had released her car back to her. I knew her prayers would give me strength to face saying good-bye to my mom.

Moments later, I was on the road with Cody to Texas. I didn't want to be rude and go to sleep on him. He was doing me a favor, and I needed his help. There wasn't much discussion between the two of us. He wasn't putting any pressure on me. And I appreciated him in so many ways.

Finally I said, "Your pretty amazing, dude."

"Who, me?" he teased. "Don't let me fool ya."

"I don't remember a lot about last night, but I do remember I followed you to your place, pretty much stalking you. I was drunk, and I wanted to throw myself on you. You could have had your way with me. But you didn't."

"I wish you would've told me about your mom. Then maybe I could have understood why you were so broken and devastated. I knew it wasn't like you to be in such a state, but it just threw me off guard," he said, keeping his eyes on the road. "I care about you, Alyx. I think about you sometimes. Actually, I think about you a lot."

His affection for me felt real. He'd been a rock, even when I'd tried to give him a hard time. He'd still stuck around.

"Well, like Mr. Murray said, I've seen a lot of people change their lives," he continued. "You say I'm a good guy—well, I haven't always been that way. In high school I was a gangbanger in training. I was real close to my thug brother, and I was following right in his footsteps. That is, till I saw him get shot right in front of me."

Clutching my seatbelt, I said, "Oh, no, I'm sorry."

"Naw, I'm straight. That was about eight years ago. Instead of dropping out, I stayed in school. From that day on, I knew I had to carry on for him, and I know your mom would want you to do the same. I don't know a lot of things about what's next after this life, but I believe there is a heaven, and I believe those we love are there. If I can do anything to help make somebody else's life easier—like a lot of the people did who came to help me get my life on track—that's what I wanna do. We gotta quit taking from this world. We gotta act like we care about somebody other than just ourselves."

I reached over and hugged him. He swerved a little bit but quickly composed himself, looked over at me, and smiled. We were connecting, and that felt real good.

* * *

Two weeks had passed. I'd said good-bye to my mother and spread her ashes over the sea between the waters of Mexico and the U.S. She'd wanted to be a part of the peace between her birthland and America. Out there on the sea, I felt God telling me to make Him my parent now. Sending my mom His way made me want to know Him more.

It was hard packing up her apartment. Thankfully, with Cody and Pedro's help, I got it done. God also gave me the strength to take care of her personal affairs.

It was a new semester and a new start. I was ready to give my work my all. I was going to try to do more than just what the homework assignment or the lesson plan told me to do. I was prepared to go further, ask more questions, dig deeper, and study harder so I could really thrive.

In two weeks, I'd done a lot of praying and soul searching. I'd learned my script lines, gained a new perspective on life, and had an understanding with God. Though I had wanted Him to lay out my life a little differently, I knew He loved me and wouldn't leave me. All I had to do was truly give each day back to Him, and I'd be fine.

Today my chapter had a meeting in our room on campus. All the love I had received from the sorors had been heartfelt. It was good to know that when you really needed your sisters, they were there.

Hayden got everyone's attention. "Listen, we gotta figure out a way to be there for each other. I know a lot of us are bummed out that we can't have a line this year, but just because we can't make new sorors does not mean we can't strengthen the bond we have with the sorors who are already in the chapter. We know some of you are struggling to keep up those grades. Some of you got serious financial problems, and some are even dealing with the loss of a loved one."

At that moment, Sharon squeezed my hand. It was so weird. She and I were connecting. At that moment it dawned on me that the reason why Sharon was so compassionate about everything I was dealing with concerning my mom was because she had lost her baby at this time last year. Deep down, I got that she was still recovering from all that.

Hayden continued. "Yes, we are a chapter that has made some mistakes, and we're all paying dearly for them. Shucks, we're suspended, but we are still Alpha chapter, and there are still some roots, spirits, and strong wills from our founders that are rooted and engrained in each of us."

"So what are we gonna do?" Torian yelled out.

"We're gonna start practicing *Robert's Rules of Order,* Torian. Let me acknowledge you," Hayden said as she laughed.

Everyone laughed along. Torian started huffing and taking it personally. Loni playfully hit her in the arm, and she finally came around. Torian grinned and raised her hand.

Hayden said, "Yes."

Torian stood and said, "Madam President, I'm just wondering what are we gonna do?"

Everyone clapped for our progress. We were a chapter ready to do business the right way—once we got reinstated, of course. I was proud of my sisters practicing correct procedures in the interim.

"I don't know right now," Hayden said honestly. "I'm opening up the floor for discussion. Anyone have any ideas of some programs and things we can do to build ourselves and build our community?"

Malloy stood and, once acknowledged, said, "I think we should mentor some young girls. We know being in college is hard enough, but just remember some of the pressures of high school." The girls all agreed. "If we reach back and let them know they can do better, we can make a meaningful difference."

"Everybody for the idea?" Hayden asked as she saw the nods. "I think it's wonderful, too. Why don't you research it and bring information back to us. Anything else?"

I raised my hand.

Hayden recognized me. "Yes, Soror Cruz."

I stood. "Maybe we should have study nights. I've been really inspired by my tutor." A lot of *oohs* and *ahhs* wailed out through the room.

"We're just friends," I said, dismissing their comments.

"Yeah, right!" Sharon yelled out. "He likes her for real."

Out of order, Bea said, "I know he better like her for real, driving her all the way down to Mexico."

"El Paso," I said under my breath.

"Order, sorors," Hayden said, getting us back on track. "Anyway, continue on, please, Soror Cruz."

"I just thought if we came together and studied once a week, twice a week, or whatever is needed, we could make sure those of us who are strong in some areas help those of us who need it, and vice versa. I don't know."

"Any comments on that idea?" Hayden said.

Loni replied, "I think it's wonderful. I tutor athletes. I'd love to be able to help my sorors instead of just the basketball team."

Retaking the floor, Hayden said, "Well, I think those are two strong programs. We can help each other academically, and we can help the community by mentoring some young girls. Sorors, if we become our sisters' keeper, if we give a little bit more than what we can take, we're gonna be rewarded. Because love is truly, after all, the most worthwhile gesture."

PERSUASIVE

"Oh, my gosh. We have to mentor these bad girls," Torian said over my shoulder as we looked at eight girls with attitudes from the inner-city middle school. These girls had been recommended for our mentoring program by their counselors, teachers, or parents.

"They aren't that bad—they're just children," Malloy retorted, being her optimistic self.

When I saw that one girl's chest was larger than mine and she was wearing a skirt way too short for her age, it looked like Torian might be right on this one.

"Well, don't just stand there, y'all," Hayden said as she pushed us toward the girls. "Pair up, choose somebody, get to know them!"

One girl was sitting down and not trying to get a mentor at all. She was popping gum loud and she had microbraids that hung to her midback and looked like they were five months old. Whenever somebody tried to talk to her, she dissed them in one way or another. I was just intrigued that she thought she could choose who was going to talk to her.

Boldly I went over to her and said, "So, you think you get to sit here during this time and talk to nobody?"

"Well, I know yo' yella behind don't think I'm about to talk to you," she said in an extremely rude tone.

In my mind, I was like, *Oh, no she didn't.* But I realized she was just a child, and I could not stress myself and get down to her level.

"What you still standing there for?" she said. "And quit looking at me like that. I told my mama I didn't wanna be in this program. If I hate listening to my teachers, I'm sure not gonna listen to y'all."

"Well, it looks like everyone is paired up. It's just me and you. So—"

"So, get to stepping. Or you could sit down there, and I'll sit right here. We don't have to say nothing to each other."

Leaning down to her, I said, "Girl, that is not going to work. Why you tryin' to act all hard?"

"Why you trying to act all down? You ain't a sistah. Of all the people in here, you the last one I want to be my mentor. What can you tell me, with your pretty, wavy hair and yellow skin? You can't understand the issues I got."

"Try me," I responded, wanting to snatch that gum she was popping out of her mouth.

"Ha! Please. I didn't pass the English test. I might have to take remedial English next year in high school. You in college and everything, so I know you pass all your stuff."

"Wrong. I may lose a scholarship because of bad grades. Next issue you don't think I understand."

"Well, I don't have no friends. Girls are jealous of me and stuff 'cause I'm fine, I'm all developed, and guys want to get with this. You know what I'm saying? It ain't my fault they still small and I can wear my mama's clothes. They ain't got to hate on me. Somebody classy like you, you can fit in and have all kinds of friends. I know it."

"Wrong again. Just like you judge me because I'm Hispanic, I get judged like that a lot of times. People always tend to say, 'Aw, you got it easy because you're this and you're that.' I don't have it easy no kind of way. My relatives don't even live in America, so I'm trying to get in where I fit in. And it's not as simple as you think. I understand being on the outside. Next?"

She slid closer to me. I was breaking through some wall I knew was going to be hard for me to knock down completely. But the layers were pulling away. She was intrigued, too. Now what was going to be the third issue she'd throw my way? Could I hit a home run with her? Could I let her know we could have a connection?

I said, "All right, bring it on, girl, what's going on?"

"This one guy I like, a lot, is not giving me the time of day. You too cute to get what I'm saying. Look at your little self. Girls may not like you, but don't even try it, I know someone like you doesn't have any problem getting a man."

Okay, she had me there. I did always have the men.

However, I had to figure out a way to make her understand that though that wasn't my exact issue, I could sort of help her with hers.

"Uh-huh. I knew you couldn't relate," she said, getting up because it was taking me a bit to respond.

"Okay, wait! Tell me your name."

"I'm Ambrosia. What's your name?"

"I'm Alyx. And . . . you're right," I said, feeling like with this slick girl I had to come clean.

"See? Told you. I'm out of here," Ambrosia said.

"No, no, no. You might want to stay. I can give you a few pointers to help you get that man."

Ambrosia froze. "Oh, for real?"

"Yeah, because that is one of my strong suits."

She started licking her lips like she was contemplating what I had to say, "Okay. You can be my mentor. Teach me how to get Brickhouse."

"Is that like his real name, fake name, what?" I pried.

"That's his last name. Everybody calls him that. Duh," she said, squinting her nose at me.

"Lose the attitude. Don't be so abrasive," I told her.

"Abr—what? What's that?"

"Hard, brash, and sassy."

"Aight," Ambrosia said. "Tell me how I get my guy."

"You can make him happy. You know what I'm saying? You got it going on. Get your confidence up. You'll see. He'll want to hang out with you. Just lose some of the attitude."

"All right," she said back.

"Write down your number. I want to speak with your mom."

"Okay." She did so.

Our session had ended up being pretty great. I was excited. I might be able to help this tough girl, drop her mean edge, and really help her embrace her dreams.

Ambrosia and I talked every day for a week. I was helping her become confident. She revealed she was scared to even approach Brickhouse regarding her affection for him. She told me he even lived two doors down, and she didn't know how she was going to make him notice her. It was actually kind of cute that she kept coming to me. And in the middle of all the boy talk, I made sure she was getting her lesson. Before we talked about the opposite sex, she had to report to me what she'd done in school that day. She seemed motivated, excited to really get on the ball and work it out. She wasn't just saying that she cared about her attitude, she was acting like it, too.

I even talked to her mom. And I was excited that her mother thought I was a good influence. Just a few weeks ago I had thought my life was empty. Then I was doing well in school myself and helping somebody else reach their full potential. I was really feeling good—till the next day when I got an alarming call.

"What do you mean you haven't seen her and you don't know where she is?" I asked Ambrosia's mother.

"We got into it. I told that girl I was listening in on her telephone calls, and I heard her talking a little too grown to that boy, Brickhouse, and I was not going to have it. She's just thirteen, trying to act like she's thirty-one," her mom said, crying. "She speaks so highly of you. Y'all have such a good rapport. I thought you might know where she is. It's getting dark now, and I'm just worried sick. I hadn't hit her since she was probably ten, but I got on that behind tonight. She is just too sassy and too grown."

"I understand," I said, trying to calm her mom down. "As soon as my roommate gets in, I'll get a ride over there."

"Thank you, girl, thank you. Y'all Betas are a blessing."

An hour later, Malloy and I were searching around Ambrosia's school and neighborhood trying to find her. It was ten o'clock—really late. Six hours since Ambrosia had left her mom's sight.

"If anything happens to her, I don't know what I'm going to do," I said to Malloy.

Malloy said, "Well, you're not going to blame yourself."

"Yeah, but I taught her to be strong and to get confident. Maybe she thought I meant she was supposed to stand up to her own mom. I was talking about the other girls who give her a hard time in school. I wasn't talking about her mom!"

"She's thirteen, not three. My mom and I have not always had the best relationship, so trust me when I say she is going to cool off and come back home. Do you have any idea where you think she might be?" Malloy asked.

"You know what? She talked about her dream guy living a couple doors down the street. Maybe he's seen her."

"You mean her mom didn't even know where he lives?" Malloy said.

"I don't know. And even if she went to the door, he might not have opened it. And I don't want to ask her mom, because she may go down there and really cut the fool. And if Ambrosia's not there, I don't want to give her hope. Let's just try to find his place."

"All right, all right, yeah," Malloy said, being the helpful friend I knew her to be.

Ambrosia's house was on the corner, so there was only one direction from which you could count two down. When I walked around the back, I was shocked to see a back window open. Malloy was in the car because Kade had called. It was good she could have her moment.

What my eyes witnessed next, I would have been too embarrassed for anyone else to see. I was so caught off guard I couldn't even stop the moment. I screamed at the top of my lungs, "No!" before things went any further.

Ambrosia turned and saw my disgusted look. She ran to the window.

"Get out here now!" I screamed to her, as if I had known her for years and wanted to beat her tail myself.

I was so passionate, she didn't dare say, "No, I'm not coming," or, "Make me," or give me any lip. She said goodbye to him and was outside with me within seconds. What in the world made her think I was for that idiotic tactic?

"What in the world were you doing, Ambrosia?" I asked her as I grabbed her by her shirt collar. "Did you think that boy would like you after giving him some?"

"Well, you said that I was supposed to let him know I could please him. . . ."

I popped her upside her dumb head. "Fool, I didn't mean that kinda way! Don't you know when boys get stuff that easy the next day you'll be the talk of the school? The laughing stock! He will never, ever give you the kind of respect you want with this kind of back-door sneaking."

"What other way was I supposed to please him and let him know I could be there for him and make him happy and stuff?"

"By helping him be the best young man he could be. Not by running all up in his face and giving him every doggone thing he wants. By making him play hard to get, by showing him what a chase is. So when you finally get him to give you the time of day with a 'hello,' he will feel good about himself. He will feel good about wanting to be with you. But you just skipped all the dating; you skipped everything and got straight to it. Don't you know what they call girls like that?"

"So? It's not like I get love anywhere else. My mama hates me," Ambrosia said.

"Your mama does not hate you, Ambrosia. She is the one who called me. She has been looking for you all night."

"Whatever. She slapped me. She don't care, and I don't got no daddy. I'm on my own, and I'm doing my own thing. And this is what I'm gonna do. And you're wrong. She don't like me."

Ambrosia started walking off as though she had said all she needed to say. She firmly believed what she was doing was okay. I had to come up with something good, something true, something real to make her understand that was not the way a young lady needed to carry herself. Nothing at all good could come from her losing her mind.

Oh, what was it going to be? How could I get her to see she was much more worthy then she was giving herself credit for? She was a diamond, yet she was acting like yesterday's trash that had been sitting out in the rain and picked over by wild dogs. Without words came emotion. Real tears fell.

She turned around. "You're crying for me." I nodded. "I can't believe you are doing that. Nobody cares for me like that. What you care if I throw my life away? My own daddy ain't never claimed me. How can some girl I just met be that into what I do?"

"Because I see a lot of myself in you, Ambrosia."

"You see a lot of yourself in me?" she questioned. "As cute as you are? As ugly as I am? I'm doing this because he won't give me no time otherwise. I know you weren't telling me to physically throw myself at him. But that was the only thing I knew to do. He got girls coming to him from every direction at school. People say I'm the ugly girl. What's the big deal if they talk about me because he goes and tells them of this little incident? I didn't deserve that treatment before, but that didn't stop them from being mean, cruel, and evil. I hate school. I hate my mama. I hate my life."

I just wrapped my arms around her. "I've been there. I've felt that. I've been so angry at myself and at God. I didn't know what I was going to do. But you know what, Ambrosia? In those dark nights, in those times, He's sent people my way who have cared way more than I thought they could, and I didn't have any understanding as to why they would! They helped me get it together. Any time you don't think you deserve what you are going through, remember that Jesus was persecuted, and He did it all because He loves you. He loves you way more than for you to sell yourself out like this. You got to know, Ambrosia, that you are beautiful."

She looked away. I could tell she was listening but didn't fully believe what I was saying.

"If a guy doesn't like you for you, that's his loss. Stay focused on turning your grades around because you want more for *you*. Remember, nobody can steal your joy. You can only give it away. Don't."

When she began to cry and sink to the grass, taking in all my words, I realized I was hitting home with this young girl who thought she was unworthy. I didn't know mentoring could really affect someone so deeply. But because I was one hundred percent in it, I was ready to make a difference—to help her find a way as I was starting to find mine.

"My teacher said we were supposed to be trying to use our vocabulary words in everyday situations and stuff," Ambrosia said.

"Okay, great."

"And I just really appreciate you, Alyx, making me believe I'm somebody," she said as I helped her up and we walked to the car. "I'm going to get it together. I'm going to go home to my mom and tell her I love her. I'm going to keep working hard in school and forget the boys. Using one of our new words in a sentence: all you've said was really persuasive."

13

BOMBARDED

"Y'all, I really don't want to go to a party," I said to Torian, Loni, and Malloy as we entered the set of our fraternity brothers, the Beta Pi Lambdas.

"Come on now, Alyx," Torian said as she put her arm around me. You've been down and studying really hard. Plus, after mentoring that hot-tail girl, you deserve a break. It's time to get our groove on."

When she put it like that, I *had* been rather serious. Most of my life, I'd been the opposite, but now that I was finally in the mode to make every day count toward me reaching my dream, I just wasn't all into what had used to really excite me. The time to shake my butt was not now.

"Plus, we got to do a lot of bonding," Malloy said as she practiced the Beta Gamma Pi stroll before we entered the door.

"Thanks for coming, y'all," Hayden announced to the four of us. She was helping her boyfriend, Creed, who was a Pi, work the door.

Hayden, Sharon, and a few other Betas were about to graduate in a couple months. As hard as it was to have real and lasting relationships in college, it appeared that whatever Hayden had with this guy was solid. He was really smiling and checking her out, all proud of his girl. That made me feel good; my soror deserved to be treated like a queen, and as mostly everybody was single in the chapter, their relationship was an inspiration to us all.

The basketball team had won—we were on a roll. And Loni and Ronnie looked like they were kicking it again. Malloy and Torian were in the middle of the dance floor with their line sisters doing a stroll. I didn't feel up to doing anything.

Malloy came and sat down beside me. "Okay, so what's really going on? Why you all somber and gloomy?"

"I don't know, I guess I've just really been thinking about my life lately. It's not that I'm not up for the party—it looks like y'all are having a ball."

"We could have a better time if you came and joined us."

"No, I guess I'm just saying I know what's important for me right now, and if I'm not working toward whatever it is I want in this life, I'm wasting time."

She just stared at me with a look that seemed proud, but I didn't really know what she was thinking, and I certainly didn't want to guess, so I said, "Whassup, what?"

"I'm just impressed. You know how awesome it is for

you to say that, for you to feel that way? Wow, Alyx Cruz has grown up. But even the President of the United States has a ball every now and then. So come on—get up off your feet and let's groove tonight."

I didn't have a choice. She yanked my arm, and the next thing I knew, I was doing a step, but I did it Texas style. Put a little something extra in it. I guess part of the old me just couldn't vanish. Before I knew it I had a crowd around me checking me out as I did my thing.

I did a Kappa Upsilon chant. "A Beta Gamma Pi girl in the house, don't you like it, don't you like it—I know you love it! A Beta Gamma Pi girl on the floor, don't you like it, don't you love it—let me show you some more!"

The Pis started howling their wolf sound, and guys were pushing over each other trying to talk to me. I was content jamming alone, but men were all around me hovering.

"You want to dance?" this Greek in a red jacket with a cane in his hand said.

He was a pretty boy—nice teeth, smooth skin, fly threads—but then he got shoved aside by a hard, fine, thick brother with gold boots. I wasn't for anybody trying to push their way up on me. I was getting shoved around, and it was not cool. It was just a dance. But brothers were seriously going at it over who would hang out with me. When I walked away from it all, I still had dudes all on my tail. I could hear them whispering behind me.

They spouted, "Dang, she's fine." "I wish I could get with that." "Look at them hips, man." "Oooo-la-la, I wish she could teach me some Spanish."

The comments were just a little overwhelming. All I wanted to do was hang out with my girls. I had used to like all that male attention, but that day had passed. So as not to be rude, I cut it off, thanked them all, told them I was tired, grabbed Malloy and Torian—Loni was already gone with her guy—and the three of us were out.

Malloy was having a pajama party at our place. We'd come a long way from a chapter that had seemed so divided when I'd first joined them last summer. As much as I loved my sorority, I never forgot I lived with the National President's daughter. It was good to see people in my chapter also give respect and reverence to the office Malloy's mom held. There were about ten of us at the party. I say "about" because Loni was hanging out with Ronnie, though she was supposed to be showing up.

As soon as we chomped down on the pizza and wings, the phone rang. Malloy started talking and told everyone to gather around because her mom wanted to speak to us. We all rushed over beside her, nearly knocking her down. It was our sorority celebrity on the line.

"No need to treat me any differently, girls. I'm just your soror," her mom said, hearing all the giggles. "And I understand big things are happening over there with Alpha chapter—some bonding going on, some mentoring going on, some grades being pulled up, and you've been attending training. I just wanted to touch base with you guys and let you know I'm very, very proud you are taking this time seriously and trying to rebuild and get stronger so you can be back on campus and get the sorority ban lifted. I can't say when it will be lifted until it happens, but I will say you're on the right road to restoring your chapter's active status."

We all screamed. We had been doing so well; really learning from the past woes of the chapter was bringing us closer. What a joy to know we were getting it right.

"I've been talking to your adviser, and of course Malloy keeps me updated. Keep pouring into one another. Keep lifting each other up. Keep being there for your sister. Only together are we the strongest. All right, have some fun tonight. Good, clean fun," our President said as we laughed and said good-bye.

Malloy had rented two girlie movies. All eyes were glued to the tube. After we watched those, of course we started talking about guys.

With a demanding look, Torian said, "Malloy, you and Alyx need to give us some tips. Y'all got men."

"I can't give you none. I don't have a man," I said, trying to hide from even myself how much I felt for Cody.

Bea said, "Whatever, girl, you got one who's crazy about you."

"Yeah, but come on," Malloy said. "We all saw Alyx handle things at the party. Right? She can tell you guys what you want to know."

"Tell us the secret!" Bea shouted out, moving closer to me.

"Yeah, can you give us any pointers?" said Dena, a Beta who was about to graduate. She admitted she had never had a serious relationship—ever.

I had to sit back in my chair and really think about

what they were asking me because if I was truly honest and told them how I felt, I would upset everybody. However, they were doing lots of things wrong when it came to trying to land a man or two.

Malloy knew me. She nudged me. "Go ahead. They're asking—tell them. Give them the scoop."

"All right, I'm not trying to hurt anybody's feelings, and I'm not at all saying I'm an expert, but there are certain things a girl should do when she's trying to attract a man."

Dena said, "Act like she doesn't want to be with them?"

"Exactly—can't be too available. Every man wants mystery and intrigue, and when I watched you guys at the party, y'all were looking around, scoping out which ones you were going to go up to. Sometimes you got to ignore them. Have a good time on your own, and the next thing you know they'll be looking at you like, 'Dang, can we do something,' and you'll be looking at them like, 'Hmmm, I'm not sure,' and that just makes them want you more."

"But that's what I was doing," Torian said. "I was over with Malloy having a good time."

"Well, that's the other extreme of it. It's great to be in a sorority and hang with your girls, but when you're looking for men, you can't be so clustered together all night that they feel intimidated to come talk to you and your crowd. I didn't get any guys wanting to hang out with me until I stepped away from y'all and danced all crazy and fun on my own. Then the hunks were able to get around me with no barriers. Nobody had to feel like they had to get through the gatekeepers or friends or sorors and stuff. Bottom line is: just be you. When you're a little interested, don't be closed off, but, dang, don't be all up in their face following them and stuff. Be warm and friendly but not aggressive and desperate. We're Betas, so we got it going on. Now we just need to act like we're the bomb, you know?"

They all nodded. We had a blast the rest of the night. And I did more individual counseling offline.

Cody was giving me a ride to dinner after play practice. I knew I'd sort of been letting him down; I didn't really know my lines. As hard as I was trying to learn them, the memorization stuff just wasn't coming naturally to me. I'd have it for a little while, but the retention was the real problem.

To add to my issues, I heard all the whispers, people second-guessing Cody's decision to put me in the lead role. The ride he was giving me wasn't just a ride to dinner and then home. I knew it was lecture time.

Finally he said, "So, Alyx, this is your opportunity. Something I know you don't want to blow."

Frustrated, I said, "What do you mean? How do you know I don't want to blow it? You're the one who thinks I have real talent at this. I never said I wanted to be an actress."

"I guess I'm just saying, Alyx, that I don't even know if you're really giving it your whole heart. How can you find out if this is or isn't something you want to do if you're not taking it truly seriously? You don't even need me for tutoring anymore because you now have the fundamentals down on how to study, to dissect what the teachers are telling you in class, and to absolutely soar past the information needed and take in even more. You are blowing tests and papers and stuff out the water."

We pulled over to a fast-food restaurant, and he turned off the car, looked at me, and said, "Before I get you something to eat, I just want to ask why you aren't giving me your all?"

His eyes were so serious and so mesmerizing. He'd been there for me in so many different ways. I didn't want to let him down, but for some reason I wasn't feeling this whole thing, and I couldn't explain it.

"You can get somebody else if you need to," I said, really meaning it. "The last thing I want to do is hinder your play. When my cohort, Charles, says his lines, a part of me wants to laugh. I don't even believe him. If you call what he's doing good acting, then I don't know, it—it just doesn't seem authentic. His big lips, his big ears—he's sort of drooling—how'd he get the lead in the first place? I came in after that whole part, remember?"

"Okay, so you're saying the brother ain't handsome, not sharp enough, not debonair enough, right? Well, imagine somebody else standing there. Who do you think is fine?" Cody said in a husky, sexy voice and leaned in closer to me.

"I think you're fine," I said to him as I moved nearer to the man who made my chest swell.

He smirked. "See, now you're playing with me."

"What do you mean I'm playing with you? You asked me a question, and I answered it. I think you're fine."

"So you're going to imagine me up there on the stage singing all those words in the love scene. When it's time to kiss him, you're going to pretend like you're kissing me? Can it feel like this?" he said as he bent forward and placed his smooth lips on mine.

My heart started racing as my mouth started moving. The physical connection of our touch made me hot. So hot that I abruptly pulled back.

"What are we doing? We can't go down this road again."

"Why can't we? Why can't you be my girl? Why can't we have something real? Then you'd imagine I'm the one up there with you on that stage when it was time to act. Your part of it won't be an act. You can really show on-stage how your heart beats for your guy. Me," he said as he playfully hit his chest two times.

Oh, what he was saying sounded so tempting, to take our relationship to a level where he'd be there for me not as a tutor, not as a director, but as a man, as a boyfriend, as someone who deeply cared for me and had no problem letting the world know it. Though all that sounded fine and good, and a lot of my sorors would have killed to have a man ask them that, I had to say no. I opened the car door and got out.

He opened up his side, slammed it, and dashed in front of me. "Wait, wait, what do you mean, no? I'm feeling something here. I know I'm not making this up in my head. This is real, girl. Come on, Alyx. Why you pulling away?"

I tried to walk around him to the left, but he blocked my way. When I tried to push him back, he used his strength to keep still. I had just been coming into my own understanding that it was okay to be alone and not really lean on or depend on anyone. My mom was gone, but I had a part of her with me. She was helping me build my own self up. To cast all that aside and need a guy or have one as a crutch wasn't cool. I needed to be secure with myself before I gave my heart away, but this dude wasn't taking no for an answer. I sighed, feeling bombarded.

GRIND

ody just stared at me with a serious look of disgust. He turned and headed back to his car. I guess getting me something to eat was out of the question, now that I had rejected him.

He drove me to my place in silence. I could tell he was really disappointed in me. I'm sure he didn't want me to say yes out of pity, but he was not a happy camper.

Trying as hard as I could not to get frustrated, I said, "Listen, if you want me not to be a part of the play, I completely understand. If that's your decision, you are not going to hurt my feelings."

"It's not that easy," he finally explained. "We have an understudy, but that person is in another role, and when you focus, she isn't as good as you. Besides, what I wanted us to have personally doesn't have anything to do with our professional relationship."

"Well, I mean, you're not even saying anything to me. You knew I was hungry, and we're not even getting anything to eat. You're just mad, upset, driving all crazy. You can't separate the two. It's clear we can't be friends."

"Can't I take it all in? Can't I deal with what you just told me? Truthfully, Alyx, you hurt me, and you want me to act like I haven't been hurt at all. Come on, girl, that's not even realistic. A brother can have feelings. I forgot all about getting you something to eat, actually, but look— you're at your apartment now. I'm sure there's something in there you can fix," he said haphazardly, like my feelings didn't matter.

I didn't know how to respond to him after that. Anything I said would probably be the wrong thing. I wasn't trying to be insensitive; I certainly did care. However long it would take him to deal with this, I was going to have to be okay with the fact that our relationship was going to be drained.

Actually, I knew, deep down inside, truth be told, that I was just as mad at myself for not being able to embrace the thought of a relationship with him. What more could any girl want? He was intelligent, gorgeous, dependable, caring, motivated, and inspiring. I wasn't saying I'd ever seen a tear in his eye or anything, but he was sensitive. Without saying good-bye, I got out of the car, and he quickly drove away, almost without me even shutting the door.

Malloy was coming out of our house at the same time. "Dang, what's up with the two of you guys? Somebody didn't seem too happy."

"Don't even ask," I huffed. "Please tell me you're going to get something to eat."

"Yeah, you want to roll?"

"Yes, I'm starving."

My mom had thankfully taken care of business and left me a little money. The state of Texas would have to pay me her social security for the next two years. Just to be able to get a hamburger and fries was a blessing.

As I chomped on my sandwich, Malloy said, "So, what do we need to discuss here? I can clearly see you need to chat. You're looking all gloomy. Y'all broke it off."

"I mean, we were never going together," I said in frustration.

"Okay, okay, excuse me. Obviously you're upset. If you want to talk about it, I'm—"

"Well, I'm just saying," I interrupted, "that I don't know what's wrong with me. I really, really, really like him. He wants to be my boyfriend, and I told him no."

"Okay, that was really smart," she said sarcastically.

"This isn't funny. Be serious, Malloy."

"Girl, I know it's not funny. If you like him, why'd you tell him no?"

"I don't know. I thought it was because I needed time to appreciate me, but I think when I get down to it and I really look at what's going on, I don't want to depend on him. What if I add him to my world and then he leaves? How realistic is it that we'll end up together? Seriously, I can see myself falling hard, and then what will I be left with when he finally wakes up and realizes I'm the last person who deserves to be in his life? I just can't get pushed aside after having invested so much. So before we can possibly get to that point, subconsciously I guess I squashed it."

Malloy looked at me like "Uh, that wasn't really smart,"

and I just hung my head low in agreement. My girl stroked my back. There was nothing she could say to lift me up, but her being there to understand felt great.

It was Valentine's weekend, and I was alone. I talked to Ambrosia, and even she was going to the Sadie Hawkins dance at her school with a new guy who liked her now that she was holding herself in high esteem. It was funny how I could give tons of advice to my little mentee and my sorors, but I had absolutely no advice for myself. I already knew I couldn't just sit there and sulk all night. Malloy was in New York visiting Kade. Why she had been so kind and left me the keys to her car after I'd taken her through so much, and had no license, I couldn't even begin to understand. She was just a friend and a great sister. She had a lot, and she gave a lot. I didn't want to let her down, but I needed to clear my head, get out of our place, and do something. I was intending to be very careful.

I ended up driving ten miles out of our city to a college club that was jam-packed. I had started drinking when I was in high school because it had soothed me and made me forget worries and troubles. I knew I shouldn't drink after that accident I'd had, but I just couldn't stay away from the club. I was trying to find a way to enjoy myself. I needed to find a way to hang out with me. A girl who had isolated lots of women until I had joined a sorority, I'd never had a ton of friends. And because boys were intimidated sometimes to approach me, I was very much often alone. Hitting a bar was my way of reverting back to my old comfort zone for solace.

When I got inside, I was very surprised and excited. I didn't see anyone I knew. No Betas, no Western Smith familiar faces, just a bunch of locals in there trying to have a good time. But then, darnit, I heard a lot of commotion over in the corner, and someone screamed my name. If I could have hid in a back closet, I would have.

"You ain't twenty-one!" he yelled.

What fool is that? I thought, hating that I was being called out.

Reluctantly I turned to face him and was shocked to see it was Ronnie—Loni's Ronnie. He put his hands all over my shirt and started feeling my chest. I slapped his hands and pushed him away. He lost his balance and fell to the floor. Seeing that he didn't have all his faculties, I then felt bad. I helped him up because I could clearly see he was drunk as a skunk.

"I got—I—I—I got curfew," he stuttered. "Currrfew—few. Need help—help me hooomie."

I wanted to say, "You knew you had curfew before you chugged down whatever has got your breath reeking, but you didn't care then. Why care now? And how did you get here in the first place?" But because the boy was barely cognizant, there was no sense being rational.

When fly music came on, he grabbed my arm and pulled me to the dance floor. He was double my height and weight and therefore easily pulled me to him. The nut started doing crazy sexual movements with his hips. I took my knee and kicked him in the thigh.

"Step back. Where's Loni anyway?"

"Loni who?" He laughed and accidentally spit in my face, "Oh, it's curfew time. My boys just left me. They left with two girls to try to get them a little piece. How are they just going to leave me here?" His words dragged just like his walk.

"I don't know, but I got to leave. I'm sure they will remember and come back to get you." I patted him on the back and wondered what in the world I had ever seen in him.

"No, no, take me with you. I got money for gas, for food, for drinks. Let's have a party." He lifted a ton of tens from his sagging pants and threw them in the air before I could stop him. The greedy locals quickly grabbed the loot.

"You are crazy. Okay, I'll take you home," I said when I realized he was alone. "You stay in the dorm, right?"

"Riiight, the dorm, athletes—that's me," he said.

I couldn't believe I had to help him get out to the car. Then I had to help him up two flights of stairs, take the key out his pocket, and get his butt in bed. I wasn't taking off any of his clothes, and I didn't care if he'd made his curfew or not. I just wanted him to get home in one piece. And as soon as that mission was accomplished, I jetted almost as fast as a jet flying over my head in the sky.

Caught up with helping Ronnie out, I had never even had time to think about how Loni would react. I thought she would have been happy because I was making sure her beau was safe. However, the next day I answered a ringing phone, and suddenly Torian was going off on me.

"How dare you get with Loni's man? That's just so unsisterly. She's your girl, and you going to do her any kind of way. Why would you—"

"What are you talking about?" I finally cut her off. "I can't even believe you going to front on me like that when you don't even know any facts."

"I know tons of facts. It's all around campus that you were with Ronnie last night."

"Of course I was with Ronnie. His drunk behind wouldn't have gotten home if it weren't for me."

"You were in his room. People saw his arm around you when you were going into his room, you coming out of there with your clothes all messed up. And he told a whole bunch of people he got it okay."

"He said *what*?" I hollered, wanting to ring his neck right then and there.

"I didn't stutter—you heard me, Alyx. And what's so bad about all this is that we have pushed way past all this stuff from the beginning of the year. You knew she liked the boy from when I messed things up and I let him come see you at our place."

"They were broken up then. Plus, I didn't even know they were an item."

"Well, they're together now, and you still got with him. Let me just say that's really tacky. Where's the sisterhood in that?"

"*Well*," I overemphasized, "where's the sisterhood in you at least giving me a chance to explain and allowing me to tell you that's not the way it went down? You just taking his word as foul? Heck, he was drunk. He doesn't remember what he was doing and where he even was last night."

In a sweeter tone, Torian said, "So you saying you didn't get with him?"

"Duh, I can't even believe you going to ask me again like you didn't hear me the first time," I said, ticked I was in the hot seat for no reason. "You know what? Where is Loni? Put her on the phone."

"She's on campus. She called me from there. People are talking about it. She was crying and all upset. Our sorors who were on the yard when this went down are mad at you, too."

"Well, heck, last time I checked, a person was innocent until proven guilty."

"Point taken. Are you going to class?"

"Yeah, I'm headed there now. Tell me exactly where Ronnie and Loni are because I need to see his butt and set this straight."

"Oh, girl, then I'm right with you. I'll meet you on the square in ten minutes."

Walking faster to class than I ever had before, I got to the square in eight minutes. I didn't see Loni anywhere, but tall Ronnie sure stood out. He had a few people listening to him mack about this and that. I couldn't believe it. Brother was either that drunk and delusional or he was just that big of a liar. Either way, there was no way I was going to let him even remotely think he could spread rumors about me. I went over—didn't say a word—and just took my knee and jabbed him again in his thigh. Hard as I could this time.

"Ow!"

"Does that seem familiar?" I said to him. "You were drunk last night at a club about fifteen minutes from here. Your boys left you. I took your tail home, trying to help you out and make sure you made it. I didn't let you drive drunk, get in the wrong person's car, mess yourself up from being eligible to play, or who knows whatever else. I should have left your drunk behind at that place if you were going to tell the world all kinds of lies about me. *You* get with *this?* Boy, never. I used to think you were a man of integrity and intrigue, but I can see now you ain't nothing but a lame jerk."

"I—I—I—I just thought that . . . ," he mumbled.

"I don't know what you thought, I don't know what you were trying to make up, but let the record show for everybody out here that nothing happened between us, last night, never. Nobody here has touched any of this." I pointed at myself, angrier than a bee who's hive had been disturbed. "That's what's wrong with y'all brothers—when you got a good thing, you're so stupid, letting what's between your legs run you off a good thing. You got my girl Loni devastated out here telling lies, trying to beef up your rep on something that never even went down. If you recall, you woke up with your pants on because I didn't touch them, and I hope she wakes up and smells the coffee and never gives you the time of day. What happened to men being gentlemen and telling the truth about situations and not trying to mess up a lady's reputation? You've got a great girl, and you're trying to brag about getting with somebody else you didn't have?"

"I'm sorry, I just thought that we . . . ," he said, trying to explain his way out of trouble.

"Please, you've lost your mind. Don't try to lie or front—you know we didn't grind."

15

PROBATION

"Hey, hey, come back! I'm sorry, dang!" Ronnie said as he tried to corner me and calm me down.

Heated, I asked, "What is it you have to say that can undo all this wrong?"

"I do feel really bad, Alyx. Thanks for getting a brother to the room. If I would have missed curfew . . ."

"Actually, I was trying to do your tail a favor. And for no reason whatsoever, you try to mess up my rep." I was so upset and frazzled, I thought of taking my literature book and throwing it at him.

Holding his head, he said, "A couple of the guys questioned me about you taking me home, and it just got out of control. I didn't say we did this and that. I just didn't say we didn't. I now see how stretching the truth was wrong."

"Yeah, but how could you do that to me after I tried to help you?"

"I'm sorry—that's why I'm sincerely apologizing. Are you going to accept it or not? My head has been pounding all day. Chuck it up to me being stupid."

I thought about the times when I had done crazy things. I needed somebody to forgive me: in days, I was going to have to appear in Arkansas criminal court for my DUI case, and I also had a hearing at the Department of Motor Vehicles for driving while intoxicated. It was going to be hard going to two different trials in one day. I was going to need mercy. I was so thankful I hadn't hit the lady and caused irreversible damage. Because no one had been hurt, and because I had told her about my mom, the lady was going to write a letter on my behalf to try to help my case. I didn't deserve her grace, but she had been moved to give me compassion.

"You better go straighten this with Loni," I said to Ronnie's somber face.

Loni suddenly came running over. "He's not the only one who owes you an apology," she said to me. "I do, too, for believing him in the first place. You forgive me?"

"I just want you to know I care about you, girl, and I would never set out to hurt you like that," I said sincerely. "The bond we're forming is just too deep. We can't fall out over no guy."

"Particularly one who isn't worth it," Loni said as she reached her hand out to me.

I ignored the handshake and hugged her instead. We started gabbing and walked away from the crowd. Happily we left Ronnie standing there alone, looking like a nut.

I had forgiven him, and she was ready to move on. We didn't need some men in our life. I only hoped her good judgment would last.

That weekend we were at the statewide Founders' Day meeting. Having had five founders, every year we'd focus on a different one. It took us five years to get through the cycle. I had pledged last year, so I had missed the first year in the cycle honoring leadership and founder Cleo Armstrong. Last year in Texas we'd had a nice-sized group there to reflect on founder Viola Roundtree when the focus was on sisterhood. This was the third year in the rotation, and we were to focus on Soror Beatrice Blue and education.

Soror Beatrice Blue was born in Pittsburgh, Virginia. She'd been an educator most of her life. The Marriott Marquis Grand Ballroom was packed, and though I thought it was hard to find white in winter, all the sorors looked lovely and ready to reflect. Hugs were given as soon as we walked in the door, and everyone was smiling and saying hello. It was a warm atmosphere I was excited to be a part of, and it really helped me take my mind off my own troubles.

The state director said, "You know our National President is from our state of Arkansas, but she has been invited to do a couple of other states' Founders' Day ceremonies, so we couldn't get her this year. However, I'm excited to preside and to give you the history of Soror Beatrice Blue, a lady who believed with all her heart that education was the key to unlocking great possibilities."

The lights became dim. We got out our purple candles, and everyone lit theirs from the one in the center of the table. We stood and said our daily prayer, watched a video on Soror Blue, and vowed to dig into ourselves in order to excel and expand our knowledge so we could increase our power and use our intellect to bless many.

The state director had us blow out the candles and then left us with these closing words. "To not be able to have an opportunity to learn and grow is a great tragedy and injustice to yourself. We are women who want to do the best we can. Though we might not be the best at everything, we can certainly try to strive to reach new heights."

It was crunch time to get ready for the big play, *Know Love.* I was now taking my role seriously, but as hard as I tried to learn the lines, they just weren't sticking.

Ben, one of the male leads, threw down his script during a rehearsal and said, "You know what? I just can't do this, Cody. Obviously Miss Cruz doesn't know her stuff 'cause she's messing me up. We open up next week and she is not prepared. We need to get another person in here for this role. Where's the understudy? Alyx is going to mess up my chances to get discovered. All the people from Broadway are coming to see this play."

Another girl echoed, "We need the understudy!"

"Why is she getting special treatment? I know all the lines. Can I just try?" said Carol Leigh, the understudy, coming from backstage. "Mr. Director, you say I don't have it like she does. I might not have her pizzazz, but if she can't memorize anything, why is that better for the performance than me delivering every line with fire? I can work on my passion."

"Carol Leigh is fine, dude," the musical director said to Cody. "I know you may like Alyx and want to get in her pants and everything, but aren't we supposed to go after what's best for this play? The dreams need to be saved for the bedroom."

Cody grabbed the guy by his shirt collar. "Okay, that's enough."

Frustrated, I said, "Listen, I don't need any special treatment. There's nothing going on between him and I. We actually haven't even seen each other lately. I just can't get the script. Mental block, I don't know."

Cody saw my despair and said, "You can get this. I believe in you."

I said, "But they are right, Cody. Look, just give it to Carol, and let's just move on."

"First of all, none of y'all are the dang-on director," Cody stated clearly.

Sharon stepped up from behind the crowd, surprising me, and said, "So you heard the man. Everyone, slow your role, and let's support her and help her get it. We all know that when Alyx is on, we've got something."

I grabbed her hand and took her to the female dressing room behind the stage. "Why did you come to my defense? Why do you care? If he doesn't choose the understudy to be the lead, maybe he'll move you up. You know all the lines, too."

Sharon said, "You know what? You're right. I do

know the lines, so maybe you and I need to get together to study them. And I like playing the antagonist role. I'm working that villain. I don't want the lead anymore. So you better get it."

Looking away, I said, "You just don't understand. This is hard, okay?"

"I understand, but Cody's right. You've got something special when you stand onstage. When you say the lines, you know we all stand still waiting for your next word. That's a true actor. That's natural ability. That's what an actress is supposed to do. You move the crowd. And just because you don't totally have it all down now, does that mean you should quit? You don't have to give the guy who believes so much in you a bad rep."

"What do you mean? I told him tons of times to get somebody else and just let me not do this, but he won't give up on what he sees in his mind. He's so stubborn. He's going to mess up his own play because he thinks I've got talent I don't have." I plopped down in the chair and held my head in despair.

"Stop that. Enough of the pity party." Sharon hit me in the head a couple of times. "I just told you you do have talent, but now you have to believe it. You've got to dig deep into your soul if you want to do this."

"So what about everything else that's going on in my mind? I'm thinking about my mom—I mean, I just lost the person I loved most in this world."

"Pour that into the person you're portraying. Transfer those real feelings to the character. The character is going through grief. Use that same emotion to be real with who this person is. And Cody—I know you feel something for him. I know you do."

"What are you talking about, Sharon?" I said, trying to play it off.

"It's obvious you both are fighting something, and I'm staying out of that 'cause you know my girl Penelope liked him. They used to be a thing, but they're not together anymore, so, hey, one of us Betas might as well snag a good man who's going somewhere. Use what you feel for Cody when you are onstage with Ben."

Frowning, I said, "Ben gets on my nerves. He makes me sick."

"Yeah, but Ben is not the character. Am I making any sense?"

"Yeah," I said and nodded.

"I'm going to send out the director to talk to you 'cause I think you got a few things you want to say to him." Sharon walked over to the door.

"Wait, Sharon!"

Sharon held up her finger and closed the door behind her. I dropped my head in my lap. My chest started heaving. I felt so uneasy. Cody was taking such heat for me. What could I say to him? Before I knew it, Cody was tapping on the dressing-room door.

"I'm in here alone. Come in."

He entered. "Sharon said you wanted to see me?"

"I just wanted to apologize. I certainly know you are expecting much more from me."

"I really am. I know it's been a tough year for you. But that's the joy of the arts. This is a getaway from your tension, strain, and strife. I don't need to name all the stuff you have going on, but I gave you this role because I really thought you could find something else—another joy in your life, something that you are good at—and appreciate that you can really dig deep into the arts and come out a rising star. But you have given me no choice but to let you go."

"Whoa, wait—I do want to try harder."

He just stood there, caught off guard by what I had said.

"Cody, I really want to succeed at this. It's just that I've had this court case—two of them, actually—and I'm stressed. I don't think they're sending me to jail or anything, but they could. The public defender I've been working with has told me to expect the worse 'cause I was too young to be drinking and driving anyway. So I'm not making up any excuses or anything, but if you give me another chance, I'm ready."

"One more chance. And you'll be all right tomorrow—I've been praying."

"You think so?"

"You'll be all right. Get yourself together. I'll see you out there in a few minutes."

As he left I bowed my head. "Lord, please help me."

"Why couldn't they just combine both the cases?" I said to the public defender, Attorney Maynor.

"Because in the state of Arkansas and in most states, DUIs are two different offenses—criminal and civil."

"So they are probably going to take my license away, huh?"

Attorney Maynor peered over his thick glasses. "I would count on it. But we've got two strong cases here. You were under the influence that night because you found out your mother had passed away. Depending on which judge we get in criminal court, it might not be so bad. Plus, we have great character witnesses here to testify on your behalf."

"Character witnesses?" I said, confused as to what he was talking about. Maybe he had the wrong client or something. I didn't have anybody there to stand up for me. I shook my head.

"Yeah, you do have some. They're sitting right back there," he said, pointing to the back of the room.

I turned around and was blown away to see Malloy and Cody. My roommate waved and gave me a thumbs-up. My theater director sat there cool, calm, and collected, but just the fact that he was there let me know he really was into me, and he really cared about what happened in my life. I knew if I was to get home—and not get thrown behind bars—I'd dive into my script until I knew it forward and backward. Cody was there for me, and that was real. If he cared that much, I certainly was going to do my part and be there for him.

The criminal court judge was a stern, older man somewhere in his sixties. Worse, he had a frown on his grumpy-looking face that wouldn't go away.

"I'm glad you're pleading guilty, and I appreciate you knowing the circumstances by which you committed this crime. But I do want to tell you that underage drunk driving is the leading cause of vehicular manslaughter, and though that thankfully wasn't the case this time, I hope you understand how grave this situation could have been."

"Yes, sir, I do," I said when my attorney told me I could respond.

"Good, because life is hard. There are going to be more tough days, but you've got to understand there's a more responsible way to deal with your pain. Hitting the bottle and just driving without consequence is a crime you must be punished for. So I'm sentencing you to one hundred public-service hours. I see here you are a member of a sorority, and you are currently mentoring a young lady. Provide me with a log of the amount of time you spend with your mentee and anything else you do through your organization. Those activities, upon my review, will count as part of your public-service hours. Also, I'm ordering you to take a six-week drunk-driving class. Because you are underage you must pay a fine of one hundred and fifty dollars. There is also a three-hundred-dollar fee for the court case and jail time."

I wanted to collapse in my seat. But my attorney helped me up.

The judged sighed. "After reading statements from your friends and members of the community, I'm going to sentence you just to the time served. So, basically, you're free to go."

He hit the gavel. I was relieved. I ran to the back of the room and hugged Malloy tightly.

"Thank you guys for coming. Thank you so much," Mr. Maynor said. "Your presence helped the judge see that this type of behavior was uncharacteristic of Alyx."

Cody said, "One down, one more to go. Looks like you got to go downstairs to your other case."

Hating that he was right, I nodded. "Thanks, you guys. You don't have to come."

"Are you kidding? We're here for you until all this is over. We are not going anywhere—except downstairs," Malloy said.

We all laughed. I walked beside Cody and just started reciting lines from the play. I didn't even realize I really knew them. But because I had released a little stress, I was able to be free, let go, and just say them.

He smiled, saying, "I knew you knew those lines."

"I'm going to study more tonight." I hated that I was letting him down.

"Thanks."

Very happy that he was in my life, I said, "No, thank *you*."

An hour later, we were on own way out of the courthouse for good. I was thankful I had gotten my license suspended for only one hundred and twenty-one days and not the maximum punishment of three years. I was happy to be on probation.

16

BUILDING

"**Y**ou should go after him," Malloy said to me as we exited the courthouse.

She didn't have to tell me twice. I gave her a really big hug. I asked her to tell my attorney I would call him and dashed over to Cody's car.

"Mind if I catch a ride? I don't have my license, but I guess you know that," I teased.

He touched my face, and our eyes locked. It was as if he was looking deep inside my soul and wanted to say more but couldn't. I couldn't hold back my feelings any longer either.

I took his hand and said, "Thank you."

"You don't have to thank me."

"I know I don't have to," I told him, blushing, "but your support has been amazing. Now, can a sister get a ride or not?"

"You might want to catch it with your roommate. I'm not heading back to campus."

I looked in the back of his car and saw a fishing pole and some bait. "You heading to the lake or something?"

"Yeah, I talked to your attorney this morning. He said he didn't think this would take all day. I just want to go clear my head before the performance."

"I don't want to intrude. . . ."

He joked, "Nah, if you cool with that, even though lions, tigers, and bears might be out there, come on."

"See? You really are an artistic type of fellow. You got that from *The Wizard of Oz*—oh, my," I said like a damsel in distress.

"See, you got that down. You know your lines fully, right, girl?"

I went around to the other side of the car and knocked on the window for him to unlock the door. During our thirty-minute drive to the lake, I recited my lines, surprising even myself at how well I could recite them. Though I had been studying them for days, it was amazing how I was really getting into the role. And as our performance dates were nearing, I certainly wanted to make sure I held up my end and made the character real to all those who'd come to see the play.

I had to admit that fishing had never been my thing. Cody started out rather lighthearted, jovial, telling me just to watch him, and he'd show me what to do. But as the sun started setting, his face got serious. I could tell something was weighing heavy on his heart, as if a thousand-pound boulder were crushing his chest.

"You were there for me," I finally said to him, tired of hearing only the birds chirping. "I don't even deserve someone like you in my corner."

"What are you talking about? You deserve it. We all need folks who care."

"Yeah, but I've put you through a lot, and yet you've always had my back. I know now that something ain't right with you, my friend. Please let me be there for you," I said as I rubbed his back.

"See, you ain't gonna make me be able to concentrate on too much of anything, you feeling me like that."

"Should I stop?" I said, caught up myself in the physical attraction I was having to Mr. Foxx.

He got up and walked toward the water. It had been a long time since I had lifted my eyes above—a few months, for sure. Not that I didn't need God in my life. Not that I didn't need Him in my corner. Not that I didn't need to be on my knees, asking for His goodness and His grace. But this time I was praying for somebody else. Not to make me a better person. Not to help me find my way. Not to take my pain away, but to help me be there for somebody else.

Lord, tell me what to say. Give me Your words. Speak through me. And I knew God had heard my cry, my heart, and my spirit. I knew Cody was worried sick about the play. The pressure to succeed at his first big show was a lot to deal with.

So I walked over to Cody and said, "You know what? You have given your heart and soul into making this performance awesome. You have gotten out so much marketing material. Radio stations are going to be there.

Dress rehearsal is next week; you'll be able to find whatever you think needs tightening."

"Man, as a playwright you get only one chance to break out. This is what I want to do with the rest of my life, but maybe I'm not any good at it," he said, doubting himself.

I took his face and turned it toward mine. "When we look above and see a plane flying in the air, we know it didn't just get up there automatically. It had to take off, pick up speed, and soar higher. Look at this as your first start. No matter what happens, you are made for this, and you are on your way to greatness. Most directors' first plays are directed by someone else. You're producing and directing your own original play out there. Cody, you're already a winner."

He embraced me. The moment lasted. I wanted him to draw strength from our touch. I believed in him, and he needed to feel that.

"So, what kind of man do you want?" Cody asked me a couple hours later as we watched the moon rise and drape across the peaceful lake in front of us.

"I don't know. I haven't really thought about it," I said—the first dumb thing that came to mind.

"So you still are that independent woman, huh? You don't want anybody?"

"I guess I want somebody like you." That completely shocked him. He did a double take and turned my face toward his.

"You gotta elaborate. You gotta explain. What are you talking bout, Miss Cruz?"

"Someone who is there for me in my darkest hour. Someone who sees things in me I don't see in myself. Someone who let's me crash their alone time. And someone who cares about my words so much I can always put a smile on their face. Someone handsome, sexy, who makes all the girls moan."

"Oh, see, now you messing with me," he said.

"Okay, yeah, I didn't mean that last part. That's not you at all." He jabbed me in the arm and then brought me to him.

Our lips met, and as the spring breeze blew across our faces, the passion and warmth in our embrace kept us clinging to each other. The next thing I knew, he was lying on top of me. We were on the little sleeping blanket he'd brought out there.

"It's getting chilly. But this feels good," he said as he looked over my face, reassuring.

"I feel good in your arms," I said, shaking just a bit.

"No, you're shivering. I need to make a fire. I need to gather some sticks. I probably don't need to stay all night with you here."

"We don't have to stay all night, but we don't have to go right now. Let's build that fire of yours and then stay and talk a little while longer. We got something cooking here—can't you feel it?"

"I'm not hurting you, am I?" he said without getting up but resting most of his body on his elbow.

"Trust me, Cody, you feel real good." My hands were resting on his back, but, boy, did I want to lower them.

But I knew this moment was about more than just physical attraction. We were connecting. He was the kind of guy I wanted in my world. And as hard as I tried to fight not wanting to get too close to anybody so I couldn't ever be hurt again, Cody Foxx was someone special.

"I really like you," he said.

"Wow, I was just thinking the same thing," I said as I pushed him gently off and rolled over, getting a little scared of what was going on between us.

"I don't want to hurt you," he said as he moved the hair off my neck and kissed it gently.

I rolled back over and lay still, looking back up at him. "What kind of girl are you looking for?"

"I don't know."

My heart sank at that moment. Of course I wanted the husky hunk to say he wanted someone like me, but he hadn't. Gritting my teeth, I frowned.

"Oh, don't give me that look. Don't be disappointed. I thought I wanted someone safe, someone who plays by the rules, someone who knows exactly what she wants out of life—but that isn't the type of woman who attracts me at all. You know the story of Penelope."

"Oh, my gosh, are y'all getting back together?"

"If we were, I wouldn't be here with you, pouring out my heart and feeling what I'm feeling. Ever since the day you walked into my tutoring session, so unsure of yourself, not even able to see how much you got it going on, I haven't been able to articulate the kind of woman I want. The more I get to know you, the more layers you reveal to me. You are helping me to grow and to care. I know God's Word says that one day when He gives me a bride, I'm supposed to lead the relationship, and I'm supposed to care about her like He cares about the church. I've just never felt anywhere close to those feelings about a woman . . . until I met you."

As he touched my cheek, glowing from the romantic moonlight, I knew as long as the Lord would allow, Cody Foxx was it for me. We built a fire and stayed in each other's arms for another couple hours. We vowed to let this thing we had going grow.

I went from a girl who didn't care about having a boyfriend to being overly into my man. I was so wanting to spend time with Cody, making sure he had everything ready for the play coming up the following week, that I did not want to go to the chapter sisterhood retreat. Though it was mandatory for all of us who wanted to be active next year—if the chapter was reinstated—I just didn't want to spend time around a bunch of women. Cody and I were into one another—our thing was getting real deep. Time spent away from that wasn't my priority.

But he'd said, "I don't want you not to be who you are. Beta Gamma Pi is a big part of that. Just because we are together, don't drop everything you had in your life for me. Go to the retreat. Hang with your sisters. Your man ain't going nowhere. I'm just getting ready for this play, so you know I'll be working overtime. It's just one night. Go."

So, reluctantly I was now in the car with Malloy, Torian, and Loni as we drove to the National Headquarters Retreat Center. With Malloy's mom as the national president, we would have some little perks. There was a meeting space we were able to use, and because it was a lock-in and all we needed were blankets, pillows, sleeping bags and such, we were good to go.

Because I'd been spending so much time with Cody, I hadn't been looking at my mail. I just so happened to have the bundled pile with me. After we arrived, I sat over in the corner of the room while the sisters started bonding and went through my mail.

I was shocked to read an official letter from President Webb stating that he was commending me—I had brought my grades up to a 2.92. But my cumulative GPA was not going to be high enough to retain the minority scholarship in the fall. I needed a 3.0.

Reading that, my eyes just filled up as if I were a sink and the faucet were turned on high. I had come so far; I had done so much; I had worked extra—and it wasn't enough? Where was I going to get the money to stay in school?

I was finally fitting in. I finally had friends. I even had a man, and I was going to have to leave? My mom had been giving me the best she could with the limited resources she'd had when she was alive. All she'd wanted was for me to be able to go to college, get a great degree, and do more than she had, continuing with my uncle's dream.

Because I hadn't taken it seriously in the beginning, because I couldn't see what an education might mean for my future, because I hadn't known that if I applied myself, I could have better choices—now it looked like it could all be taken away. And that hurt.

The Chapter President spotted my tears. Hayden came

over and said, "Okay. Now we are all pouring our souls out, and you've been a little distant, and we see you opening mail and stuff. What's going on, girl?"

I didn't feel like talking. I needed to leave and be alone, but then the letter slipped out of my hand. She read it and consoled me. "Don't you worry about it, girl. We are going to find a way to get this all figured out. You've been helping each of us lift up our self-esteem around here this semester."

Dejected and discouraged, I said, "Yeah, but I guess too little, too late for me."

"When you got family, it's never too little or too late. We need you to be encouraged," she said, trying to give me hope when I felt hopeless.

My letter got passed around the room. I had wanted it to stay private, but Hayden was right: we were a sisterhood, and they did care.

Hayden said, "If we can't get enough money, we will pray for you, Alyx. We are in this together, and we are going to figure out a way."

"I don't need for you guys to do that. I just need for you guys to take care of yourselves. Go get some men," I teased, trying to step out of my sadness.

Individually they each came over to me all that night, hugged me, let me know they were in my corner, and told me great things that were going on in their lives because I had entered their world. At the end of all that love, I guessed I believed Hayden. Someway, somehow it would all work out. I was a part of a family, and no letter could destroy the love we were building.

GRADUATE

After the opening night of the play was successfully over, I stood there onstage completely humbled and in awe of the standing ovation I was receiving. I had studied the lines so much, I practically knew them out of order. I knew everybody's part. I felt like a real thespian, but nothing had prepared me for actually being onstage in front of a real audience. They had devoured the performance I was giving them as if they were hungry and I was the only supplier of food. They had wanted to get something good from the play, and we had delivered in a big way. Cody's play had everyone in the house on their feet.

It was so fun. It was so good to be a performer I couldn't wait until the next night to do it all over again. Had I found my calling? Had I finally stumbled across the thing that made my heart race? Had I established what I wanted to do with my life? Had I discovered the way I wanted to contribute to society? I couldn't say my performances the next few days would be as dynamic, but I was certainly excited to try.

"You were so good," Hayden said as several of my sorority sisters surrounded me with private applause backstage.

They had come to see Sharon and myself in the opening-night performance, and there were all kinds of beats bopping and Beta Gamma Pi chants going in the hall. They were so supportive. Obviously they were proud.

"That's my roommate, y'all. The star of the evening is my girl," Malloy said as she hugged me tight.

Loni said, "This is for you." She handed me a dozen roses.

"That is so sweet," I said, smiling wider than a kid with their braces off on the first day.

"Well, we are just proud of you. All of us are really proud of you," Loni said with a pitiful look on her face.

I could tell she wanted to move past the tension we'd had before. Though I had truly thought we were past it, she obviously still felt bad about believing her jerk boyfriend over me initially.

I took her to the side and said, "You got to let it go. We're moving on from that. That's done. We're straight."

"But are you sure you can really forgive me? Here I was mad at you, telling stories, and passing on things that weren't true. I was really defaming your name, and that's not what sisters are supposed to do. Alyx, from the bottom of my heart, I'm sorry."

"It's okay, girl. I'm not perfect either. I don't get it all right, but I want you to know you got it going on, and you don't have to settle for some guy who treats you less than what you are supposed to be." I hoped she realized Ronnie didn't deserve to carry her purse, much less have her time.

"Yeah, I learned that. While our sorors have been taking your advice getting lucky—catching a man here or there—I let mine go. I'm excited to stand on my own, you know? I'm going to be a senior next year, and I really don't have time for drama."

"I know that's right, girl." I put my hand in the air to receive some dap, and Loni obliged me.

"Drama is supposed to be onstage. Yes, I remember you used to tell us you didn't know what you wanted to do, what you wanted to be, but, girl, you made me cry watching you," Loni said with that proud look of accomplishment my mom had used to give me.

After all the difficulties she and I'd had—not big stuff, but bumps along the way—it meant so much to have her full support. Maybe that was confirmation that maybe I had found my calling. Was this an affirmation that, yes, the stage was it for me?

"So are we going out to celebrate, or what?" Torian said, coming between us. "Enough with the tough stuff—let's have some fun."

"Tough stuff? Girl, we straight," Loni said, smiling in my direction.

Torian said, "Good. Well, are we going to party?"

Actually, I had my mind on other things, on other people. I looked around and tried to find Cody but wasn't able to locate him.

Torian noticed what I was doing and said, "Girl, he's probably interviewing with the press, or somewhere talking to a whole bunch of people. He'll hook up with you later. Hang out with your girls. You got through your first big performance with flying colors. Let's celebrate."

She was right—I had. But even though I appreciated that they wanted to be with me, I needed to be with him. This was his play. It was a success. He had been so worried. I needed to tell him it had been great, and a part of me longed to hear him say I had been great, too.

I thanked my girls for the offer and hugged each of them for their support. "I'll meet with you all later."

Malloy winked at me. She gathered them toward the exit. The crew looked disappointed, but thankfully they understood.

I just couldn't stand there and wait until Cody found me. Though I had several people come up to me, stop me, and tell me how much they enjoyed the play and my performance, I couldn't let that detour me from finding my guy.

Sharon came over. "You looking for Cody, aren't you?"

"Yes. Where is he, girl?" I said, happy someone could help me find him.

She stood in my way. "First, let me say you should come out with us—hang with the girls this time."

"I just told Malloy, Torian, Loni, and everyone that I am gonna hang with my man. I want to be with him tonight."

"He might be busy," she said in a weird voice like she knew something I didn't.

"Okay, you're being a little evasive, and you're freaking me out the way you're talking. What do you know, Sharon? What—what's going on?"

"I'm not saying anything. I'm not trying to start anything. I'm just saying come with us. Hang out. You did great. You were awesome."

"I couldn't have done it without your help, but I want to be with my guy. What's the problem?"

She turned around and looked at a closed door backstage. Then she looked away and then back that doggone door. Something was up.

I probed, "What? He's back there? Who's he talking to? Some financiers, some school officials, some New York producers? Who? What? Tell me!"

"Just come on." She tugged my hand. "Okay?"

I jerked it away. "Let me go."

With her hand on her hip, she said, "You don't want to go in there."

I went to the door and turned the knob. It opened. Before I opened it all the way, I could see Cody in Penelope's embrace. I took a deep breath. My heart started racing so much it felt like I had just run a marathon or something and needed an IV.

Certainly what I was seeing wasn't what was really going on. He was backing away as I saw her lips really close to his ear. She was doing more than congratulating him for an excellent job. When I was about to interrupt them and ask for an explanation, I froze in my tracks.

Penelope said, "You don't want to end up with that

girl, the way you value education. She needed you to tutor her, for goodness' sake. You need a woman who's able to help expand your vision. Not someone who is needy. You got to pour so much energy in her you aren't even able to pay attention to your own dreams and goals. You don't need her to pull her down."

"Naw, you don't need me to do that," I said, wishing I could take back each word and just leave him alone for good.

"Shucks," Penelope said loudly, knowing I had ruined her rap.

I walked out of the room and heard Cody say, "Penelope, I'm sorry, I wasn't trying to give you the wrong impression, but she's my girl. Alyx, come here! Come here!"

"You did such a good job today," Ben said to me as I tried to get away.

Penelope ran past me. Cody grabbed my hand, and I tried to pull away from him. He kept the grip and pulled me back into that room.

"Look, you don't have to explain. I saw what I saw. She made a great case. You were wrapped up in her embrace—go after her. Leave me alone," I said, sounding pitiful.

"No, we're not going down this road. You're not going to get this wrong. You're going to hear me out. Yes, I hugged her. She's doing an internship for the ABC Little Rock affiliate evening news, and she brought them here to review the play. They have been advertising it all week—because of that exposure, it was sold out. I was thanking her, and she started making a case as to why she was better than you for me."

Sighing with relief, I uttered, "I'm sorry I misjudged the moment. I just don't want to bring you down. Your woman should contribute to your dream. I can't offer you as much as Penelope can."

"You offer me more. Having you in my life motivates me to succeed. My heart belongs to you, and, truth be told, I could write the best script or direct the best play, but if I didn't have an actress that got up there and did her thing, it wouldn't mean anything. So can we leave the 'you're not good enough for me' conversation for good? Can we move past that? Can we get over that? Can you come and give me some sugar? Dang!"

With a big, huge smile on my face, I went to his arms. I kissed his ear. "Thank you for helping me find my way. I love being an actress."

"And I love you," he said.

Had he said the big three words? Yep, he had and I was stunned. I took a deep breath, trying to process his response. I'd never heard those words from a man, and hearing them was not taken lightly.

Other cast members wanted to talk to him. I encouraged him to give them a second. This was his time. He needed to be off and take in all the glory and accolades there were to give.

The play *Know Love* was about two people who defied the odds and always gave more to each other than they wanted for themselves. Our relationship was a mirror of that experience. He'd wanted so much for me, and now, as bad as I wished we were alone, I wanted him to have his moment. Finally he agreed, and I was awfully proud to see a big investor smile and then whisk him away.

It was graduation day. All the sorors were so emotional. Not only did we have a lot of girls graduating—including our Chapter President—but the first African American governor for the state of Arkansas was speaking at the graduation. I hadn't known Hayden, Bea, Sharon, Dena, and Audria that long, but I knew them to be sorors who wanted to make a difference. They wanted to graduate and get out in the world and even get their master's or really get to work in their chosen careers and take to heart the real meaning of Beta Gamma Pi. They wanted to leave the world better than they found it. Even though my time to graduate wasn't until next year and I didn't at all know how I was going to stay in school to make that happen, today wasn't about me. It was about being there for my girls and listening to our governor give a speech I knew would really make a difference.

Governor Floyd came to the podium and said, "Graduate and excel. Yes, I know this is the high point of your life for many of you. Mothers and fathers out there in the audience, I know you're excited that your child has reached a milestone in his or her life, and although this is a very important day, I am talking to the graduates and those who are close behind them. Yes, graduating is something you strive for or reach hard for, but this is only the beginning. What is burning inside you, longing to come out? What do you want to give to the world? How can you take the education you learned here and educate even more with the knowledge that this institution has given to you? Have your college days helped shape and mold you? Have the mistakes you made here ensured that when you get in the real world, you are done with childish, foolish, crazy things? Yes, life isn't promised to you, but right now you are living, and you're breathing, so promise yourself you are going to make the most of it—be positive every day. Know you can achieve and are equipped to do so. Whatever your major or study, once you get out there in the world, tap into that knowledge. Use it to propel you toward greatness. I see a lot of young people—not you guys here at Western Smith College, but a lot of young people—who feel that college is just a place to party, to hang out at, to participate in a group or club at, to socialize at. But these people never really understand the value of an education. Once you know better, once you know in your heart what is right and wrong, once you're able to reason and think for yourself, you are armed with what it takes to break down the barriers people say you can't reach. How do you think I got to be the governor of this great state? Many said I couldn't, and many will say you can't, but we must turn off those voices that do us no good. We must turn on the ones that can cheer us on."

He went on to talk a little longer, but I so wanted to stand up right then and say amen—and I wasn't even Baptist—because Governor Floyd seemed to be speaking directly to me. I had made a lot of mistakes. I hadn't taken my education seriously, and now I was in a position where I was paying for my past actions—my scholarship might be taken away. Yet, I still knew I could be something. I knew I could do something. I knew now

172 Stephanie Perry Moore

that my education was important, and I still had a chance to get it right. A graduation ceremony was a symbol of acquiring information from a set course. It was a ceremony that signified that you had moved on from that education, and now that I understood what my life was about, I had a desire and dreams I wanted to obtain. The partying was okay, but it had its place, and I planned to seize all the opportunities set before me. In some way I was also a graduate.

PROMISE

"So you ladies think you got it together now, huh? Well, I hope you learned your lesson: the school's giving you guys a full pardon. You're ready to get your chapter active again, effective next year," Malloy's mother said in our chapter room.

It was amazing that a full year had passed since I had been a part of Alpha chapter. And now that Hayden had graduated, we were without a leader. In front of our regional coordinator, our chapter adviser, and our National President sat ten ladies from Malloy's line, plus Trisha—who wasn't graduating—and myself. We all looked like lost puppy dogs.

"Okay, so I guess there's no way to prove to me you're ready to get your chapter back. I don't care what the university says—I'm the one who needs to give the okay to the National President. Somebody better speak up and tell me why y'all deserve a chapter," our adviser said.

As much as Torian loved to talk, she didn't say a word. Loni was opinionated and strong-willed, too, yet she was also quiet. Malloy was known for going toe to toe with her mother, but, shockingly, she didn't say anything either.

So I stood and gently said, "Madam President, I was not in this chapter when they went astray—"

"Yes, that's right. I remember I met you last year at the National Convention. You were transferring. So your year has been okay?"

"My year's been quite eventful, actually, and I don't think I would have made it through without the sorors in this chapter."

"Well, I know Malloy loves having you as a roommate, but do you want to speak to why you ladies deserve a chapter?"

"I cannot say that I know exactly what the founders were thinking in 1919 on this very soil when they decided to start this organization, but I can say that the five core principles they believed in—leadership, sisterhood, education, Christian principles, and public service—are all evident in Alpha chapter today. I know a lot of people often think the only way to pledge someone is to haze them and make sure they're not paper, that you cannot be a part of the sisterhood unless you take some kind of beating. But since I've been in this chapter, I've lost everything—I've been emotionally beaten, and only the sisterhood was there to help get me through it. Collegiate chapters across the U.S. are supposed to be the core, the foundation of our organization, and we deserve our chapter back because Alpha chapter is where it all started. And sometimes you have to lose something to be able to completely understand how much you need it, how much you value it, how much you treasure it, and I think not being active on the campus has allowed every member of our chapter, past and present, to understand that we need to be here. We need to be out in the community making a big difference; we need to be on the campus as leaders. We need to have our letter symbols displayed so folks know the Betas are about the business of making the world better. We won't let anyone down again."

"Wow. If I were in this chapter, you'd sure get my vote for Chapter President," Malloy's mom teased.

Shocked, I shook my head. "I think I want to nominate your daughter for that position."

Torian stood beside me and said, "I concur wholeheartedly. Malloy is the glue that holds us together. She never wanted to participate in hazing, even last year."

"Malloy? Wow," her mother said.

"Mom, there's no way I can top Hayden."

"You're the glue that holds us together," I said to Malloy.

Torian leaned in and said, "Because of who your mom is, you know the rules. We need a leader with that knowledge."

We went on debating the point for a few more moments, and her mother went out of the room with the regional coordinator and our adviser and then came back and granted us our chapter. We elected officers; the unanimous slate read as follows: Malloy—President, Alyx—

First Vice President, Torian—Secretary, and Loni—Treasurer.

"By the power invested in me as Beta Gamma Pi's National President, I am honored to install Alpha chapter back on campus and declare that the four officers are duly installed and can begin campus activities August first."

I was First Vice President of Alpha chapter—such an honor and a privilege. I knew deep in my heart that if I found the funds to stay, I wouldn't let the chapter down. How was I gonna make that happen though?

"So you know we gonna get to have a fall line," Torian said to me as she, Loni, and I walked across campus. "And we gotta get ready."

"Don't even look at me crazy, girl. We are not going down that road again. We are not getting no underground line."

"I'm not saying we need to have an underground line or anything. I'm just saying we need to be strategic about who we want to pick," Torian said. "We got all summer. We gonna think of something they can legally agree to. See—look at that group over there looking eager," Torian said, pointing at a group of freshmen. "That one, with her chest hanging out for all to see, rolls her eyes at me every time I see her. I am not picking her."

"See? You're making it personal," I said.

"Just because we can't haze them doesn't mean they can't respect us. Let's keep it real."

"Remember, we're not even back on the yard officially yet," Malloy said as she came up behind us.

"Your girl is trippin'," I told Malloy.

"Yeah, being off the yard for a year makes it sort of hard. And look at those freshmen over there." Torian pointed at the same girl for Malloy to see. "That one girl in particular with her chest all showing. Her skirt can't get any higher, or we'll be seeing her underwear. She's stuck up so much I know she wants to be a Beta."

The girl was actually cute, but Torian was right—she did look a little too hot, and not in a good way for the yard.

I said, "She's walking over here."

"Oh, no, she better turn around. Don't she know we're Betas? She can't just speak to us without an invite," Torian said.

"Girl, you are crazy! We ain't even back on the yard, and you are trippin'," I told her.

"Well, you talk to her. Come on, y'all," Torian said as she grabbed Malloy and Loni and left me.

"Hey, I just wanted to come and introduce myself. I'm Cassidy! I wanted to meet you and your sorority sisters. Can you call them back over here? I don't know if y'all are back on the yard again. The word is the National President is here, and y'all are gonna have a line, like, now, so I just wanted to introduce my—"

"Okay, slow down!" I said, cutting her off. "My sorority sisters had to take off. I'm Alyx Cruz. We're not sure about any lines or anything like that. We are officially off the yard still. However, we are hoping to be back. It's good to meet you."

"Well, any advice you can give me? Anything you can tell me? I ain't gonna say nothing to nobody. I'm gonna keep it to myself. You can tell me a secret, girl. Hook a sister up! What's up? What's up?"

Okay, this chick was really ghetto fabulous, and that wasn't a bad thing, but it wasn't Beta Gamma Pi style. Apparently the way I looked at her made her think she'd done something wrong.

"What? I'm too much, huh? All my friends said you real cool for an outsider. You should understand a girl like me. I'm a little rough around the edges. You're a little different for Beta Gamma Pi, too. If you can be a Beta, there's hope for me. Why everybody gotta be so clean-cut? So stuck up?"

"Okay, I don't think you want to use that tone or say anything like that, because when you're trying to get into a sorority, you got to get voted in. And I'm not considered an outsider."

"So I gotta change who I am to try to fit being a Beta?"

"You need to first understand that being a Beta isn't something you should need to change into. You shouldn't have to change you, and you should definitely not want to bring down the organization."

"Oh, why you sayin' it like that? I thought you were cool and stuff."

"I *am* cool. You came to me off the record, and you're asking me to give you some advice, and I'm just keeping it real. If you don't want to hear it—"

"Naw, naw. I do. Most people talk behind my back and say this and that. Can't even say it to my face. So I respect what you got to say."

Now that I had her undivided attention and she was ready to listen to me, I found it hard to say, "You dress like a slut." How could I tell her she was too loud and obnoxious? "Most of my chapter is not interested in letting a girl like you into our sorority"? But seeing the sincerity in her eyes, I could tell there was really something in her that reminded me of myself. I hadn't been a shoo-in from my line back in Texas either. They'd had to look deeper. Our founders would want us to give every girl a real chance, and just like academics hadn't been all that for me when I'd gotten here, the sorors had sat me down— they hadn't given up on me. True, they hadn't had a choice—I was already a Beta—but there was something to be said about showing compassion and not judging folks. If I was going to be the leader of the line, I was going to have to rise above and give girls chances when most people would think they didn't deserve one.

So I said to Cassidy, "Just look deep inside yourself. Keep supporting our events, do community service, try to be the best Cassidy you can be: and, um, look us up in the fall."

"Thanks, girl!" she said and she gave me a big hug. "I ain't gonna tell nobody we talked. You are the bomb! Thank you!" Then she swished away.

Everyone was moving out. Malloy was keeping her place; it was a town house her dad was buying. She was going back to New York to do another internship with that designer, and although I wasn't sure how I was going to be able to stay in school, I was praying I could find some kind of job over the summer that would give me money— or apply for a loan. I was planning to stay around, get my head together, and figure it out.

"You're gonna be okay," Malloy said to me by the door on her way out. "I know—Loni and Torian and I are not here this summer."

"Oh, that's ok—you're going to New York. I don't know. I have no choice but to focus on what I need to take care of."

Malloy said, "You can call me anytime. This is our place. I love you, girl."

"I love you, too," I said.

"Ah—it looks like you're not gonna be too alone."

"What do you mean?"

"Look who is pulling up," she said as I peered around her and saw Cody.

A big smile spread across my face. My girl said she'd give us privacy. I told her to be good in New York, and then my comfort blanket was gone. Then, when my guy came in, I knew I truly wouldn't be alone.

"I got some good news and bad news," he said.

"I don't think anything could be any worse than me not knowing how I'm gonna pay for school next semester."

"So, which do you want to hear? The good news or the bad news?"

"Good news."

"Well, you know I've been meeting with those investors about financing my play in other cities. I'm sorry, baby, that I haven't been here to be with you. I've missed you. They're gonna finance my play. They want to take it to four states: Texas, Louisiana, Mississippi, and all over Arkansas."

"Are you serious?"

"Yes, your man is going big-time. This is steps away from Broadway. The actors and actresses they want to use are so good. It's all coming together."

"I am so excited for you!" I threw myself into his arms. "That is certainly good news. So I wanna know the bad news." I pulled away.

"We're not going to be together."

"Physically?"

"Right. We won't physically be together. I'll be on tour with my play, making some money. I'll be here this summer though. I'll finish up with my master's, and then I'll be able to leave."

"Oh, I might be able to go with you. I'm not a Broadway actress or nothing, but maybe I can work on the play if I can't stay here."

"Well, you didn't let me finish with the good news."

"What are you talking about? Your play got picked up—let's not act like that's not good news."

"These financiers, they also have a foundation that helps support the arts. Long story short: they loved your performance, and you have a full, one-year scholarship to get a degree in the arts."

Tears just welled up in my eyes. Finally I was doing the right thing, and God was blessing me. All I wanted to do was focus on my own dream, not hold back my friends, give other people opportunities, and appreciate my education—and of course be in love—and He was giving me all that. Alyx Cruz was gonna be okay after all. Just like my mom had said, I was gonna be able to make it. I, too, planned not to let God down.

"Now look at you. You're all emotional. This is good, right?"

"This is great, Cody. Thanks for caring about me so much. I miss you already."

"We'll have the summer. You just tell me that when I leave you're not gonna forget me and go get you one of these young college boys."

"Look at you sounding all old and stuff," I said as we laughed. He picked me up and twirled me around. We kissed. "You are in my heart."

If the Beta Gamma Pi founders could have seen me now, they'd be smiling. I had my act together. I had a pretty cool guy at my side. I cared about making a difference with everything I did.

"When we take your play to Broadway—I'm gonna be starring in it because I'm taking my education seriously. I believe in my man. I believe in me. I believe in everything Beta Gamma Pi wants me to be. Does that sound crazy?"

"No, it sounds like my girl is the bomb."

"You believed in me the whole time?"

"Yeah, but now you believe in yourself. All right, tell me again: you're mine, right?"

"Yes, I'm your girl." I kissed him and then thought he still needed reassuring. "I promise."

Beta Gamma Pi, Book 3:
Act Like You Know

Stephanie Perry Moore

ABOUT THIS GUIDE

The following questions are intended to
enhance your group's reading of
Beta Gamma Pi: ACT LIKE YOU KNOW
by Stephanie Perry Moore

DISCUSSION QUESTIONS

1. Alyx Cruz is hated by the Betas because of how she looks. Do you believe it is right to judge people because of their skin color? What does the saying "Don't judge a book by its cover" mean to you?

2. Alyx moves in with Torian and Loni and ends up making a date with Loni's ex. Do you feel Alyx should have gone out with the guy, or backed out like she did? What are lines that should not be crossed in friendships?

3. Alyx house-sits for Malloy and agrees not to have a party at her place. When life gets rough for Alyx, was she wrong to go against her word and have people over, anyway? What are positive ways to deal with the pressures of life?

4. The chapter calls a meeting and tells Alyx she is giving them a bad name. Do you think it was wrong of the Betas to set one of their own straight? What are ways to help someone in your group know her actions are hurting everyone?

5. Alyx finds out her mom has a brain tumor. Do you think it mattered that Malloy and Sharon rallied around her? How can you be there for someone who receives devastating news?

6. Alyx is about to lose her scholarship. Do you think she was wise to give her tutor, Cody Foxx, a hard time? When you are in need, should you let go of your ego and receive help?

7. Cody wants Alyx to try out for his play. Was Alyx right not to try out for the play at first? When others see things in you that you don't see in yourself, should you listen?

8. When Alyx goes to visit her mom, her mom encourages her always to do her best. Do you think this was a turning point in Alyx's life that made her inwardly want to excel? What motivates you to achieve?

9. At a party, all the men are on Alyx, and all the Betas ask Alyx for advice on men. Do you think the secrets Alyx shared were helpful? What are other ways a young lady can attract the opposite sex?

10. The Betas start a mentoring program, and Alyx's mentee, Ambrosia, is off the chain. Do you think Alyx's counsel helped this troubled young lady learn her self-worth? Where does your self-worth come from?

Stay tuned for the next book in the series,
GOT IT GOING ON,
available in January 2010, wherever books are sold.
Until then, satisfy your Beta Gamma Pi craving with
the following excerpt from the next installment.

ENJOY!

BENEVOLENT

*Y*eah, I know I got it going on, and even with all the eyes rolling my way, I'm not gonna feel bad about that. My almond-toned skin is glazed to perfection. My five-foot-seven body is slim in all the right places, and I know how to work it. Every guy at this Student Government Association back-to-school party is checking me out, including the fine, commanding SGA president, Al Dutch.

Al Dutch—yes, he wants everyone to use his whole name all the time, saying he plans to run for a political office one day, and we need to remember him—is a ladies' man. He looks, walks, and talks like money! You know the type—the one who's confident, cocky, and always has the smile of a future heir plastered on his face. The no-worry, got-much-loot look in his eyes. His skin glows like he has slept on the best satin sheets and used the finest body oils all his life. All the men wanna be him. All the girls wanna be with him. And all the ladies in the room saw him checking me out. Heck, yeah. It was game time; I was flirting hard.

Western Smith was your typical college, rich in history in our great state of Arkansas. We had everything at our disposal: a good football team, excellent academics fit for intelligent men and women, an amazing Greek life, cultural campus events, and even the place where I fit in most—the band.

I was drum major my sophomore year. Now that I was a junior, I had switched gears and was going to be doing something different. I was now captain of the dance team. One would think my life was perfect, but my reputation wasn't the best. Though I didn't care what people thought or said about me, I knew I wanted to make the line of Beta Gamma Pi. Three years ago when I'd first come to college and was at a probate show, I'd seen the girls stepping, and I knew I really wanted to be a Beta. Plus, their sorors in my hometown of Natchez, Mississippi, had helped get me through my preteen and teen years. Because they had cared, I wanted to do the same for someone else and become a Beta. Their scholarship was why I was in school today.

In high school, I had researched the sorority. I found newspaper clippings of where the five founders had started the group on this campus back in 1919. I'd even taken a tour of the National Headquarters about thirty miles from campus. The more I'd looked into what the Betas were all about—leadership, sisterhood, education, Christianity, and public service—I knew four out of five of their mission points were dear to my heart as well (the whole God thing wasn't really for me). But I knew to be a Beta, I had to either clean up my act and hope they would vote me in or cancel my dream altogether.

DATE DUE

AUG 3 1 2010	NOV 0 1 2011	
NOV 1 2 2010	MAR 1 3 2012	
	MAR 1 3 2012	
NOV 3 0 2010	SEP 1 0 2012	
JAN 0 3 2010	OCT 0 1 2012	
JAN 0 6 2010	OCT 0 5 2012	
MAY 0 4 2011	OCT 1 9 2012	
MAY 0 5 2011	JAN 3 1 2013	
SEP 0 8 2011		
SEP 2 3 2011		
SEP 2 3 2011		
OCT 0 6 2011		
2 5 2011		
OCT 2 5 2011		